The Lady's Great Escape

SAFELY IN SCOTLAND, BOOK 2

ALLISON B. HANSON

ARE YOU SIGNED UP FOR DRAGONBLADE'S BLOG?

You'll get the latest news and information on exclusive giveaways, exclusive excerpts, coming releases, sales, free books, cover reveals and more.

Check out our complete list of authors, too!

No spam, no junk. That's a promise!

Sign Up Here

www.dragonbladepublishing.com

Dearest Reader;

Thank you for your support of a small press. At Dragonblade Publishing, we strive to bring you the highest quality Historical Romance from some of the best authors in the business. Without your support, there is no 'us', so we sincerely hope you adore these stories and find some new favorite authors along the way.

Happy Reading!

CEO, Dragonblade Publishing

Chapter One

London, April 1814

SETTING DOWN HER quill, Thea Rockledge went to her door to listen to the voices below. It was unusual for her brother and his friends to return home so early in the morning. They generally arrived closer to noon.

Thea shook her head, reminding herself that there was only one friend now. The rest had scattered years ago. Only Lord Billings remained. Perhaps Stephen's only true friend, for Stephen had nothing else to offer anyone but friendship.

Only a year younger than Thea, Stephen had become Viscount Percival at the unfortunate age of six and ten. When he lacked the responsibility and skills necessary to continue the title's success as her father had.

In the ten years since, she'd watched as her brother spent all their money—including her dowry—before turning to selling off anything else he could to cover his gambling debts. There was nearly nothing left.

Their home in Mayfair was in disrepair. Any furnishings of value had been sold by her brother or stolen by the fleeing servants as payment. Only two maids remained and they were paid directly from Thea and were told to tell her brother they stayed on for room and board alone.

Her brother didn't even keep ledgers on the properties any

longer for there were no funds coming in from the country estates. Nothing had been invested to plant anything and their tenants had all moved on to greener pastures, quite literally.

The country homes were rented out to gentry, but lately their rent had been used to maintain their homes instead of providing income to the viscount.

Thea thought when they were completely out of funds it would force Stephen to stop gambling, but she'd been very wrong.

Peeking over the railing into the foyer she saw two large men rather than Stephen and Billings.

"Look at this place. There be nothing here o'value, it's already been ravaged." The man kicked a broken clock with his scuffed boot. That clock had belonged to her mother. Thea had broken it herself so it might be spared, but now it was too late for the clock. Too late for everything.

"Flint, won't be happy if we come back empty-handed. Should we check upstairs?"

Thea backed away into the shadows, so not to be seen.

"No bother. Men like 'im would'a purged the upper floors first and kept the receiving rooms pretty for appearances. There won't be anythin' upstairs."

Despite the man's rough speech, he wasn't wrong. That was exactly how Stephen had managed his debt. She wouldn't be surprised if he'd sold off his very bed and slept on the floor if it would offer another night of entertainment.

Thea kept her rooms locked at all times, but she'd come home to find the locks broken once or twice. A crystal inkpot had been taken along with her best dress. Fortunately, she didn't have any funds in her room. She had learned that lesson early on.

"We should go tell Flint. 'e'll probably want us to come back 'ere later to hand out a beatin'."

Another beating. Thea's stomach twisted uncomfortably with the memories of the last two she'd tended. When she'd begged Stephen for the final time to stop this.

He'd cried as he had when he'd been a boy. He'd promised her that was the end of it, but he wasn't strong enough to keep that promise, or perhaps it was that his sickness was more powerful than a mere mortal could defend against.

She realized afterward, when he'd returned to pawn more of their goods while still bearing the bruises, that her brother was beyond promises. He was not in possession of himself.

Much like a drunkard sought out his next drink, Stephen could not turn away from the thrill of the tables. It was no longer something he did to pass the time, or an innocent amusement, but it had become a dire need that controlled him and lured him to the worst of gaming hells as his credit was denied at the more reputable establishments.

He was completely lost to it. And as with anyone suffering the loss of their will to something, it changed the way a person saw things. And provided justification for things they previously would have thought reprehensible.

Soon after the men left, Stephen and Billings returned.

"It doesn't look like they took anything," Stephen said, kicking the same clock. She wondered if he even remembered the significance of it. The memories it held.

Billings sniffed. "You've got nothing left for them to take."

"That's not entirely true. There's one thing here that still might have enough value to get me out of this business with Flint."

Thea didn't know what he was speaking of. She didn't keep her funds in the house so there was no danger of Stephen finding them.

"Stephen, no. Surely, there must be some other way," Lord Billings said, as if recalling a conversation they'd had before arriving home. "The last time Flint threatened you, we were able to run off to Cawdor Castle. Perhaps we could hide out in Scotland as we did the last time and wait until it blows over. Flemming's dower cottage made for a comfortable enough hideout."

"You think Flint will just forget I owe him ten thousand pounds?"

Ten thousand pounds? Thea clenched her hands into fists. Who had allowed him to borrow such a sum? Anyone with half a mind would know Stephen didn't have that kind of money. In fact, he had no money at all. He'd already gambled everything away.

And the last time they'd run off to Scotland, Flint hadn't simply forgotten the debt. Thea had seen it paid with her own money. But *ten thousand pounds…?* She didn't have that much. At least not until her next book was finished and sold. And even then, she might not make enough to cover it.

Her books had been picking up in sales, but she couldn't ever be certain when interest would sway to another publication. Writing was a fickle beast.

If there were some guarantee it would be the last time he would rack up such debt and he would stop gambling, she might have found a way, but she feared there was no hope for her brother.

"We can't go to Scotland. I suggested it to Flemming and he said he needs to stay in London for the rest of the Season. Cawdor Castle is closed up until he returns. Besides, I don't fancy a trip all the way to Inverness."

"I imagine he's not pleased with you after what happened last time with his maid. But still, a long trip to Scotland would be better than a short trip to a grave. Which is what you'll face if you don't come up with the blunt."

"I told you. I know how to get it." He let out a resigned sigh.

"But Thea… She's your sister."

"She's a spinster who spends all her time hiding in her room writing letters to people she never visits. She's been nothing but a burden. If I could marry her off to someone with a fortune, I would, but she has never come out. And there is nothing for a dowry. No one will want such an aged oddity."

She frowned. At seven and twenty, she was aged. And, yes, she did spend all her time in her room writing, but it wasn't letters or journals that took up her time. She was a novelist and a fairly popular one at that.

Using a male pseudonym, she had collected a fair sum in payment for her nine novels published in the last eight years. And her newest manuscript was due in a matter of months. She had a deadline looming, but now she worried she would never have a chance to finish the book at all, let alone by the date she'd promised.

Who did her brother plan to marry her off to? She pictured the thugs who'd been in their house earlier and shivered.

"Flint has said he will take her off your hands to clear your debt?"

"He wants to see her first, to make sure he can make the sum back."

Thea stifled a gasp. She'd misunderstood and somehow it was even worse. There would be no marriage. She was to be sold.

"He doesn't plan to marry her?" Billings said. Thea wondered if the man was really so naïve. But then he'd shown his lack of intelligence in whom he chose to befriend. For she didn't think there was a man more worthless than her brother.

"No. But her virtue will be worth a pretty penny. I'll have to get her a proper dress, and lord only knows how I'll get the ink stains cleaned from her fingers."

"How will you get her to agree? She's not just going to go off willingly for such a thing."

"I'll slip a hefty dose of laudanum into her food at dinner."

Thea realized then her sweet, fun-loving brother was completely gone. The grief hit as if she'd just gotten word he'd died. In many ways, he had. But instead of one single shock of death. Stephen had been slipping away for many years.

She backed away and rushed silently to her rooms. She hadn't even closed the door before she started to formulate a plan. She would go to the MacLains' home. The couple had been servants at Percival House before her brother let the staff go.

Thea had hired them herself to see to things she could not.

She'd funded their son, Robert's, education and now the young man was Thea's solicitor. The MacLains took care of business for her. Delivering her manuscripts to her publisher and securing her accounts.

Thanks to her having to pay off Stephen's debts last year, she didn't have enough to purchase a home yet, but perhaps with the sale of her newest book she could.

Packing as quickly and quietly as she could, she took the back stairs and went out the servants' entrance without meeting up with her brother. Rather than take a hansom cab, she walked, staying off the main streets where her brother might see her if he'd already come looking for her. She wanted to be sure there was no way her brother could track her to the MacLains' home.

She knocked on the back door of the MacLains' tidy house she'd purchased for them with the proceeds of her first book. Mr. MacLain opened the door with a smile.

"Have you finished it already, lass?" he asked as his gaze dropped to the bags in her grasp. Her arms trembled from carrying them all this way. She'd left so much behind, but she had a few changes of clothes and all her writing supplies and manuscripts. They were the most valuable to her.

"No. I'm so sorry to have come here. But I desperately need your help."

As she'd rushed from Percival House, she'd started devising the next step of her plan.

She couldn't stay in London. Her brother was desperate and wouldn't stop until he found her. She needed to leave as soon as was possible. She needed to go far away where her brother could not find her. She had the money to rent a place, but not many reputable people would rent to a single woman. Mr. MacLain could do it, but Mrs. MacLain was not in the best of health. Robert had a business to run, and wouldn't be able to leave London at such short notice.

They would, however, be able to secure a carriage to take her where she needed to go. But where?

"Whatever ye need, lass. You know we'll help," Mr. MacLain said in his Scottish brogue. It gave her an idea.

Scotland.

She'd never been there as the Percivals had no holding there. But she knew someone who lived there. Or rather she didn't know him, for they'd never met. But she knew Lord Flemming had a dower house that would be vacant for the rest of the Season. That would give her enough time to finish her book and come up with a long-term plan.

"I need to procure a carriage to take me to Cawdor Castle, in Scotland. And I need to leave immediately."

A few hours later, having made her escape from London, she was on her way north. To freedom.

Chapter Two

S HEAMUS BUCHANAN, MARQUESS of Flemming, squinted up at the sunny day after exiting the House of Lords. He had done his duty to his best friend, Reese, by casting his vote in the earl's favor.

"Ah, you look like you're ready to quit London this very minute," Reese said coming to stand next to him.

"Maybe not this minute, but soon enough." He frowned.

"What keeps you then? *Nuit Noire?* You should sell the place," Reese suggested.

"And if I did where would you spend your evenings?" Shay asked. It was not the first time Reese had shared his disapproval for Shay's business. A business he hid from polite society.

"You know the risk. We may have lofty titles, but we're still Scots, and they would love nothing more than to run us back to Scotland so we don't have a say in what happens."

"At the moment, I would love nothing more than to return to Scotland. I have managers that can run *Noire* for me while I'm away. But I told Percival I wouldn't be returning home until the end of the Season." The whelp had a thirst for the gaming tables that would never be quenched. Last Season, Shay had thought him just a poor player with a lust for winning—despite his skill not being up for the score. Shay was ashamed to admit he'd taken advantage of the man. But after he'd ended up with Stephen Rockledge in his castle for all but five months, and put his staff at risk, Shay had decided the man was too far gone. His need was a festering fever that would never go away.

The man wouldn't ever be able to pay all that was owed. No matter how far north he went or how long he hid.

"Ah. Good thinking. The last time he chased after you to Cawdor, it seemed he never planned to leave."

"I hear he owes Flint a large sum. I'm guessing he's looking to hide out until it blows over. I still don't know how he got out of it last time."

Flint wasn't the kind of man who forgot a farthing of debt. Which meant someone must have paid it off. But he didn't know who, or why. Not that he cared enough to ask around.

"What are you planning to do?" Reese asked.

"I told him I wasn't returning home. I didn't say anything about visiting a friend not far from my estates."

"Finn and Lily?" Reese guessed correctly.

Their friend had married a lovely woman and they'd had a son the previous January. They hadn't bothered coming to London this Season. Apparently, there was nothing here that compared to spending time at home with his family.

Shay wouldn't know about that. He didn't have a family. He'd been living on the streets in Inverness until someone had tracked him down to pin the title on him. A great-uncle had fallen ill with no other heirs. Shay had gone from a starving lad of eleven summers to being the heir of the marquess in a day's time.

"I am Uncle Shay, Willie's favorite uncle, I might add." Shay had never thought he was missing anything in not having a family. Not until Finn married and Shay was able to see the happiness practically beaming from the man whenever he'd spoken of his wife and son and the new babe on the way.

Shay began to wonder if having such a thing might fill the emptiness he never realized he had in his chest. But finding someone in London was beyond him. These debutantes were out to find a wealthy husband at any cost. They were not above treachery to secure their futures.

He blamed society rather than the lasses who employed such devious plots. For they were given but a short amount of time to find a proper match. Too many Seasons put them on the shelf and they were considered less desirable.

Shay thought he would prefer a woman of mature years as opposed to a lass who'd just left the school room. The few he'd spoken to, stared owlishly at him when he spoke.

Either he'd frightened them or they weren't able to translate his rough Highland brogue. Either way, Shay thought returning at the end of the Season to meet what women were still left might be a better tactic.

"The lad is little more than a year old," Reese argued. "He doesn't know who the blazes you are from anyone else."

"You insult the young earl's intelligence. 'Tis no wonder I'm the favorite."

Reese rolled his eyes, which was quite common when they were together.

"Safe travels. Tell everyone I send my best," Reese said before adding, "And thank ye for your vote. It means a lot to me that you stayed."

There was not much he would not do for Reese and Finn. When Shay had showed up at Heriot's school in Edinburgh, a skinny lad, with the speech of the streets still thick on his tongue, he'd been a ripe target, but Finn and Reese stood at his back against the older boys and Shay would never be able to repay their kindness.

After a hearty hug and a slap on the back, Shay gave a nod and headed for his home across the park. He stopped and changed course when he spotted Percival and Billings moving quickly through the park as if looking for something—or someone—they'd lost. He could only hope whoever it was that had escaped them, would never be found.

THEA STEPPED DOWN from the carriage, drawing in the fresh air of Scotland and breathing out all the stress she'd been carrying during the trip.

The dower house was exactly as she'd expected. Empty.

But it was also clean, roomy, and comfortable. It would be the perfect place to hide from her brother while she finished her latest book. She would need to find her way to the village to hire someone to cook and take care of the household things. Such as reminding Thea to eat.

She often forgot about all else when she was deep into her stories. Her brother never noticed. Shaking her head, she brushed off all thoughts of her brother. Her trip north had given her time to shed a few tears and come to terms with the man he'd become.

After her few bags were brought in, Thea paid the driver and watched as he rode off, leaving her there alone. She turned to take in the view from the front porch. The house sat on a small rise that looked out over the village and rolling green fields. Up on another hill sat a formidable castle, it's light-colored stone glowing in the sun. Cawdor.

Huge mountains rose high in the distance, their peaks still white with snow despite it being late April. She thought she might want to include a trip to Scotland in her newest novel. It would be fun to add different scenery to her books.

She frowned thinking how sad it was that writing about something fun was the closest she ever got to actually having any fun. But things might be different now. Or soon enough.

If she had the money to buy a house it could become a home. Perhaps she would live in a small village like the one sitting below the cottage. She might make friends.

A twinge of guilt twisted in her chest at the thought of making a happy life while leaving her brother to fend for himself. She was still worried about her brother, despite all the reasons not to be. Instead of thinking about him, she did her best to keep her mind busy so she wouldn't be distracted.

She was setting up her blank pages and ink on the desk by the window in the drawing room when someone knocked on the door. She froze for a few quick beats of her heart before she went and opened it.

A robust woman and a slender man stood on the porch looking more than a little surprised to see her.

"Good day," Thea greeted them, wondering who they might be, and what lies she would need to tell them.

"Good day to you, my lady," the woman said after a silent conversation between the two people. "We are..." She looked toward the man who took over the explanation.

"We are servants from the castle. We saw a carriage come through and thought to come see who had arrived. The marquess did not write to tell us we were to expect any guests." The man spoke while his expectant gaze went past her shoulder to the empty room behind her.

"It is just one guest," she answered, the question she thought he truly wanted to know which was if she were alone. "And I didn't get a chance to tell the marquess I was coming before I left town. But..." she swallowed before telling the part that was a lie, "he had offered a standing invitation some time ago. I never had the chance to take him up on it though. I hope it is no trouble. I'm to understand he's not returning until the end of the Season. I was just going to write to let him know I had arrived." She was near to babbling and bit her bottom lip to stop it from moving.

"Very well," the woman said, though she seemed uncomfortable.

"I'm Thea Rockledge," she announced, thinking that knowing her name might help. "Has the marquess ever mentioned me?" Of course he hadn't. She'd never met the gentleman and he'd likely never heard of her.

"We are John and Anna Murray. The butler and housekeeper of Cawdor," he said with some pride. The thin man smiled at

Thea while the woman was clearly not yet sold on her story. Thea continued on, hoping to convince her.

"It is a pleasure to meet you both. I only plan to stay a couple months, I'll need to hire a maid of all work to see to things here. If you have anyone in the area you might recommend, I would be appreciative."

The two shared another look before the woman spoke.

"And what brings you to Cawdor, Miss Rockledge?"

In this, Thea could tell the truth. She'd only been here a quarter of an hour, but she was already enamored with the beautiful views and clean air.

"I hope to purchase a home in the area." Just as soon as she had enough funds after she sold the book she had yet to finish. Her future depended on her being able to finish her book. And to do that she needed peace and quiet.

"Hmm." The woman pressed her lips together into a strained smile and bobbed a curtsy. "Then we welcome ye. We should be able to spare a maid to take care of your needs during your stay. I'll send her down straight away to help ye unpack. Will you be joining us for supper in the castle this evening?"

"No. I won't be a bother. I plan to stay here at the cottage during my visit."

"Very well. Please let us know if you need anything else."

"I will do that." She would not. She was already a trespasser. She wouldn't take advantage of these kind people.

It seemed she was not the only person who was lying though. For if Flemming told Stephen the house was empty and closed up, that had not been the truth. Could it be that Lord Flemming didn't want her wastrel of a brother planting himself at his home? Thea couldn't blame him one bit.

With the interruption over, Thea got back to work. She organized the pages she'd completed, reading through the last few so she might pick up where she'd left off weeks ago before she'd learned of her brother's nefarious plans for her future.

Thea shook her head. She needed to focus. She couldn't think of Stephen and what might have happened in London when he found her missing.

Had he been upset? Had he been angry? Perhaps he had yet to even notice. Whatever he was doing, it was no longer her concern. She would finish this book as quickly as possible and use the proceeds to buy herself a home. Somewhere she would be safe from ever having to answer to a man ever again.

Chapter Three

"MUST YOU LEAVE so soon?" Lily Lockhart, Duchess of Granton, asked Shay as he secured his bags to his saddle. Shay had enjoyed his visit with Finn, Lily, and their son William, but it was time for him to move along and leave the family to their privacy.

It had nothing to do with the fact Willie had taken to climbing all over Shay anytime he sat down. The lad was small and it was fun to make him laugh until he was out of breath. He especially liked when Shay pretended he hadn't noticed the boy was hanging on his back.

"It has been two weeks, a fine length of time for a visit, I'd say. Nay too short, nor long enough that you are counting down the seconds until I depart."

Finn shook his head. "That would not happen. You know you are welcome here always."

"Aye. And I know that's because I don't overstay." He winked at his dear friend. "Not all of us hate being alone, Finn."

Shay knew how much Finn despised solitude. He'd come from a loud, happy family and lost them all one by one. Until he'd married Lily it had seemed the duke hadn't fit in anywhere. London was too busy, while Scotland had been too lonely. Until his wife and son came along.

"Enjoy your peace and quiet," Finn said with a nod.

Shay would surely do that. Unlike Finn, Shay preferred being at home alone. The only place where he could be himself. Where he didn't have to worry that he might make a mistake and his secrets would all come tumbling out.

Even after all these years, being with people presented a risk that he might share the truth, or worse that he might want to. But that couldn't happen, for if it did, the life he'd made would be over and he would lose everything.

Shay made good time getting to Cawdor by the late afternoon. He turned over his horse to a groom and went inside to see Mrs. Murray hustling everyone about for his arrival.

"No need stirring everyone up, Mrs. Murray. I will not waste away if I have to wait for a meal." That was not something he'd had to worry over since he'd moved to Cawdor as a small boy. He never needed to go hungry as he had when he'd been a lad living on the streets of Inverness.

Some nights he would still dream of that pain in his belly, but he never needed to worry about where his next meal came from, it was always presented to him in a timely manner.

"'Tis no bother to see to ye, my lord. We are happy to have ye home." Mrs. Murray gave him a fond smile. She hadn't seemed to age since the day he'd met her. Back then she'd loved fussing over him and plying him with treats. It seemed she still enjoyed taking care of him. It was just in her nature.

"It's good to be home. I'll be in the library until dinner is ready."

She nodded and left him in the foyer as her husband took Shay's bags and passed them over to Cragen to take them upstairs. Shay would send for his valet to return home from London, but the footman would do until then. It wasn't as if Shay needed to be dressed in his finest for sitting about the house with a book.

When he'd first been brought to Cawdor, he'd been asked to wait in the library. He'd stood in awe of the tall shelves filled with books. His mother had read to him when he'd been very little and while he'd not learned to read he wanted to know every story in that room.

He'd been given a tutor and became an eager student. Then he'd gone off to school and filled his mind with as much as it would hold. All these years later, Shay couldn't say he'd read every book in the room. Some were dreadfully boring and others were in languages he didn't know. But he had read most of them.

And now he had a new novel to add to the shelves. One he'd brought with him from London and couldn't wait to start reading. He'd already shrugged off his coat and waistcoat. His cravat had been gone before morning was over. All the formal clothing was one thing about being a lord he didn't particularly care for. He much preferred the easy dress of the lower classes. He didn't enjoy all the attention put into his wardrobe. He just wanted to be comfortable and clean.

He poured a glass of whisky and stood at the window looking out over the grounds. It still amazed him that he was responsible for all of this. However, his gaze fell on something that shouldn't be there.

"John?" he called for the butler who came in immediately.

"Aye, m'lord?"

"Why is there smoke coming out of the chimney of the dower house?"

"Ah. I imagine Frannie is cooking dinner for your guest," the man answered as if that were a perfectly reasonable explanation.

Shay's eyes went wide. "I have a guest?"

John smiled softly. "Aye. Did ye not get her letter? She said she was to write ye to let you know she'd arrived, but I'm guessing you were already out of London before her missive arrived."

"She?" He had a *female* guest. Women sometimes became quite brazen in their search for a husband, but he never expected to have one show up unannounced and take over his dower house.

"Miss Thea." John's smile returned as if he were talking about his own daughter. "Ye know Frannie has not been well since last year, but the lady has sure been kind to her. And she's paying Frannie more than she earns here."

"My guest has stolen my employee?" Shay was growing more irritated, and he'd not even met this *Miss Thea* yet. He'd wanted to be home where he could relax, not have to entertain some woman who had apparently wooed his staff.

"Anna said it would do the girl good to have a fresh start somewhere else. Miss Thea doesn't want to move so far from here so Frannie will be close to her ma and brother, but will still be able to make her own way if Miss Thea keeps her on."

"Mayhap I should go speak to my guest to see what her plans are." Whatever plans she had, he wanted to ensure *leaving his property* was at the top of the list.

Shay set off for the dower house which was set some distance from the castle that was not quite far enough away to need a horse. When he arrived he was breathing heavily from both the length of the walk and the quickness with which he had completed it.

He rapped on the door, although he really shouldn't have had to. It was his house after all. This stranger didn't belong here. But he waited until Frannie opened the door.

She'd always been shy, but after what happened last year, she'd become downright skittish. Especially around men.

"My lord," she said without meeting his eyes as she ducked a curtsy.

"I'd like to meet my guest," he said, adding what he hoped was an encouraging smile when Frannie's eyes went wide and anxious.

"Oh. She is writing in the drawing room and doesn't like being disturbed."

Shay laughed at that. "I'm sure she won't mind if I interrupt."

Frannie moved to the side so he could enter. He went straight to the drawing room door and opened it.

The woman inside was not at all what he'd expected. He'd imagined a debutante, a young girl dressed in a pale dress, waiting for the opportunity to trap him into some kind of arrangement. But Miss Thea was too old to be a debutante. Not that she was old. She was surely younger than him, but not by much.

Dressed in a blue gown, her blonde hair was pulled up on her head in a hasty bun she'd likely done herself. Tendrils had escaped and were teasing her face. Not the artfully done curls the women thought made them look coy in the ballroom, but actual messy locks that had escaped of their own accord.

She paid them no mind as the quill in her hand scratched swiftly across the page. She barely looked over when she dipped the quill in the well to gather more ink on the tip. The inkwell showed the many droplets from her constant returns. Her fingertips were stained and there was a smudge on the side of her nose that should have looked ridiculous but somehow didn't.

He thought her eyes were brown, but wasn't sure because while he'd made it a good three steps into the room, she'd yet to look at him. He had all the time needed to take in the room. Pages and pages of ink-filled paper draped over every surface.

It was clear enough by the sheer amount of them she was writing a book—no a novel—he corrected as he noticed the larger pile of pages already stacked on the table by the window. Two quires of blank paper sat at the ready on the corner of the desk. It was either a novel or the woman was mad.

He cleared his throat and did so a second time when the first attempt did nothing.

As if waking from some dream-like state, she finally glanced up at him.

He'd been correct. Her eyes were brown. But that word was not adequate to describe all the different colors of gold, amber, chocolate, and dark earth that swirled about her irises. And since when had he cared to notice the multitude of shades brown could be?

She blinked then sucked in a quick breath as if shocked to

learn she wasn't alone despite the fact he hadn't been quiet as he'd entered.

"Who are you?" she asked.

He was surprised by the smile that came to his lips at her question. She hadn't sounded rude as much as inquisitive. But it was the question for him to ask the person who'd invaded his home, not the other way around.

"I'm Lord Flemming. Who the hell are you?"

Chapter Four

T HEA GASPED THEN stood up so quickly she knocked over the inkwell and the abandoned teacup on the desk. Liquids went in two different directions. Both puddles heading for her pages.

She grabbed up the paper before it was too late. Wiping the edge on her gown to clear away the bit of tea that had hit its mark. Her attempt to save it, smeared the ink, but it was otherwise legible. So long as the typesetters could read it, all would be well.

Breathing out a sigh of relief, she faced the man who was waiting for an answer to his question. She considered lying for a moment or two but decided to go with the truth instead. Not because she was beyond deceit, but that it would only delay the inevitable.

It wasn't as if he would allow her to stay. The only thing she could hope for now was that he wouldn't tell Stephen she was there.

"Theodora Rockledge."

"Aye. I know your name. What I don't know is *who* ye are."

"Isn't a person the sum of their name?" she asked with a tone she could only describe as haughty. Perhaps if she continued to stand her ground she might have a chance of winning.

She looked the man over once more. He was huge. Taller

than her brother, wider as well. He had the blackest hair and the bluest eyes. She blinked so not to get caught in them.

He shook his head. "Not even a wee bit. A name means very little. Especially if the name is not recognizable."

He was not a lackwit like Stephen's other friends. If he was truly one of Stephen's friends. For he'd lied to him about coming here.

She let out a resigned sigh. There was nothing for it. She hated to be the damsel in distress, but she would need this man's help.

"Very well. You know my brother. Viscount Percival."

If Lord Flemming had tried to hide his look of distaste, he did a poor job of it.

What she hadn't expected was to hear a gasp and a whimper from the doorway where Frannie stood, looking white as a sheet. What had this man done to Frannie? She was clearly terrified.

Without a second thought, Thea walked closer to the maid standing in front of her. She held no weapon but she would protect this poor girl the best she could.

"Don't worry, Frannie. I won't allow him to hurt you," Thea promised. "What kind of monster takes advantage of his staff?" she accused the man who was staring at her as if she were daft.

When Frannie also blinked and shook her head, Thea thought perhaps she had misunderstood.

"You're afraid of him?" Thea pointed to Lord Flemming.

"Goodness, no. He's always been a kind man."

"Then why do you look so horrified? Who are you afraid of?"

"Ye're brother hurt Frannie," Lord Flemming explained. "I would never be inappropriate with my staff, but I imagine ye think all of us Scots are naught but barbarians."

She shook her head. "I don't judge you because you're Scottish, but because you are a man." She couldn't help the look of disdain she sent his way.

"I thank ye, for your protection, my lady. But it is hearing your brother's name that gave me such a fright. Please say he won't be coming here."

"No. At least, I have gone to great lengths to avoid such a thing," Thea said, hoping that she hadn't caused this woman more harm for coming here.

"Forgive me for saying so, my lady, but he is a right devil. Lord Flemming would never hurt me. He is a good man," Frannie said earnestly.

Thea glanced over at the marquess and let out a breath.

"It appears we have gotten off to a poor start, my lord. My apologies." She turned back to Frannie. "I'm sorry for whatever my brother did that caused you this pain. I fled London to escape my brother. He doesn't know I'm here." She looked back to Lord Flemming. "He *can't* know I'm here. Please."

This shocked Lord Flemming, at least a little bit. He tilted his head, likely waiting for her to explain. But it was Frannie who spoke up.

"He ruined me," Frannie said so quietly, Thea wasn't sure she'd heard her correctly. It took a moment for Thea to comprehend and then she reached for the girl just as she broke into tears.

"I'm so sorry, Frannie. I had no idea." In truth she hadn't realized her brother was capable of such a thing, but a man who would drug his sister and sell her off clearly had no honor at all. Thea felt foolish to have been surprised.

The girl swiped at her nose and firmed her shoulders. "He didn't force me," she explained. "But I hate him. He pretended to like me. Made promises. I believed him, but it was all lies to get me to trust him. To…" She shook her head. "I thought he was kind, but he used me."

"That is why he was not invited back. I don't want him or his kind in my home again," Lord Flemming said.

It was clear he meant her when he'd said, "his kind."

"My brother owes a man named Flint ten thousand pounds. He's sold everything of value in our home. The furniture, the silver. There's nothing left and he's become desperate. He planned to give the man the only thing left in the house that might have value." She swallowed and looked away, hating that speaking it out loud made her feel dizzy.

"You?" Flemming guessed correctly.

Thea nodded. "I overheard his plan to dose me with laudanum and give me to Flint. My virtue to cover part of his debts."

Frannie was the one to hug Thea this time. "We can't let him take her, m'lord."

"Frannie, can you leave Thea and I alone for a few minutes so I can decide what is to be done?"

Frannie backed away but stopped to whisper in Thea's ear. "He's big and gruff, but he's a kind man. You're safe with him, or I'd not leave ye with him."

"Thank you, Frannie." Thea was thankful for the girl's protection. But Thea thought Flemming would likely think differently of her than he did Frannie. Thea's blood was tainted.

When Frannie was gone, Lord Flemming began walking around the room as if he were thinking. She would rather hurry this along one way or the other.

"If you wish me to leave, I would understand. I would just ask you to not tell my brother I'm here. I'm seven and twenty, well past my majority, but my brother is still considered my guardian in the eyes of the courts. He would be able to force me back home and I will not face such a fate."

"I take it you have a plan? Other than living in my dower house for the rest of your days."

She breathed a sigh of relief. He was willing to listen at least.

"Yes. I have a man who handles my business affairs. In a few months I will have enough funds to purchase a property here, and I will send for him to come facilitate the acquisition. I enjoy the area and would like to live here permanently."

"Your brother gambles the way he does, yet you have the funds to purchase a property?"

"I will soon enough. I earn my own money." She couldn't help but glance at the pages strewn around the room. Lord Flemming must have noticed as well for he picked up the first page from the pile on the table. That was where she collected the pages that had completely dried. But of all the pages he might have perused, that one was the most damning.

She saw him pause and then his blue eyes flared with recognition.

"Theodora Rockledge." He pointed to the page and smiled. "Theodore Stonecliff." He laughed. A booming sound of amusement that made her smile. "How clever."

She remained silent, for if she'd been so clever, he wouldn't have been able to figure it out so easily.

"*The Case of the Golden Feather.*" He looked around the room. "This is a new book?"

There was no sense in lying. The evidence was right there before him.

"Yes. I'm Stonecliff. And yes, this is my newest novel. My publisher will be expecting it in two months' time. I will be paid when I turn it in, so I've been working night and day to complete it. It's so peaceful here and without the constant distractions of my brother's debauchery I've been able to complete more than half of it."

"You are one of my favorite authors," he admitted easily.

"Well, thank you." She'd never encountered an admirer of her work in the flesh. She found it quite… embarrassing. "I'm sure you're surprised to learn I'm a woman."

"Only in that women are not usually allowed to take part in such activities."

She laughed despite the tense situation.

"Oh, I'm not allowed to do this at all. Thus the *nom de plume*, and the secrecy. My man of business sees to the delivery of my work and collection of my fees. This," she gestured to the room, "is the part no one knows about."

"Except for me."

She frowned and let out a breath before squaring her shoulders and nodding.

"Yes, Lord Flemming. You now know all my sordid secrets.

Including the fate that awaits me if you decide to tell my brother where I am."

"I have no intention of telling your rotter of a brother where you are. That's your own business."

She felt her shoulders drop in relief, that particular weight alleviated.

"And what of my other business?" Again she gestured to the room.

"I'll tell no one."

"Thank you." She glanced at the pages that were surely dry enough now. "Then I shall pack and be away. Please accept my apology for invading your home."

"What will you do now?" he asked.

"I'll go to the village to find a room to let until I finish and have the funds for Mr. MacLain to come north to help with the purchase of a cottage." She hoped someone would rent to her. She didn't need much assistance from a man in her daily life. But things like this could be dangerous.

"You will have the funds to purchase a home in two months?"

"Yes. I had enough previously but…" She shook her head.

"You paid off Percival's debts last year," he said sounding almost accusatory. Or maybe it was as if the answer to a complex puzzle was finally revealed.

"I did."

"But you won't do it this time." It wasn't a question, but she felt the need to explain anyway.

"I don't have ten thousand pounds. And I daresay even after this book is done I won't make that much."

The man cursed at the sum and she couldn't blame his surprise.

"I have no idea why this Mr. Flint allowed my brother to run up such a sum. He has to know Stephen has no money. And…" She stopped. The marquess didn't need to know any of this. Yet, she'd already told him so much and felt she could trust him.

What a silly thing to feel when hardly any man she'd ever known had been trustworthy in any way.

"And?" he pushed, seeming very interested in her answer. Maybe it was his sincere interest that compelled her to answer.

"And… even if I had it, I don't know that I would pay it anyway." That sounded rather harsh, so she defended her decision. "It isn't as if paying the debt would make him stop. I don't think anything can make him stop. His plan to give me to Flint proves how desperate he's become to keep playing. He is no longer the brother I once knew. I'm worried for him, of course, and I still consider ways I might help him, even after I made a promise to myself not to. This… *sickness* he has succumbed to is worse than death. For if I had truly lost him, I would grieve and move on. Instead he was taken away from me day by day, hour by hour. Which is torture. I don't know that helping him, would really help him at all. And if I do nothing and something horrible happens, I fear the weight of the guilt I will bear the rest of my days."

Her throat grew tight, but she had given up on crying over her brother. There was no use for tears. They did nothing but make her nose run.

"You have a firm grasp of the situation. As you say, it is a sickness. Just as it is when a person has a thirst for gin that can never be quenched, your brother lives only for the thrill of the game. Even when he wins it brings him little satisfaction. For he no longer plays to win. He plays simply to feel that hope of winning. You canna help him. Your money would only prolong his agony."

His words seemed to provide some absolution, and the freedom brought on the eruption of unwanted tears, and she couldn't make them stop.

$$\text{——}\cdot\text{——}\textbf{❧}\text{——}\cdot\text{——}$$

Chapter Five

I F THERE WAS a greater hell than seeing a beautiful woman cry, Shay didn't know of it. Thea was different than any women he'd ever met in the ballrooms of London. She had lived a difficult life. She was educated in the harshness of the world. Yet, she'd found a path to take care of herself not many women of the *ton* would be strong enough to forge.

Seeing her break from his words, forced him to act in a way he never would with an unchaperoned woman. He took the necessary steps to stand in front of her and pulled her close. He wrapped his large arms around her thin, heaving body and stroked his hand over her back in what he hoped was a soothing manner.

"I'm sorry," he said. Either for his words or for her pain. He would allow her to choose. She only seemed to cry harder, but he didn't think it was because of him. This formidable woman had been carrying such a weight on her slim shoulders and she needed to weep, to cleanse her soul of this darkness.

He knew it in a way only a person who had done such a thing would know. And he had broken down and cried away his own guilt, many times over the years.

Eventually, her sobs slowed and she managed to catch her breath. He let go of her only to reach into his pocket to fetch his handkerchief. This kind of crying left one a mess. But he hoped she felt better for it.

"I apologize," she said. "I've made a mess of your home as well as your shirt."

"Neither are beyond repair."

He looked about the room at the pages laid out to dry on their own. She must write too fast to sand them properly and stack them as she went. He recalled the speed with which she had been writing when he'd arrived. If she'd finished half the book in the time she'd been here, it would not take her long at all to finish the other half.

He would likely have a new Stonecliff novel in his hands by winter. He enjoyed sitting by the fire with a glass of whisky, reading late into the night as the snow stacked up outside. After his years of being cold and hungry, he made sure he never suffered either offense ever again.

Thea stepped away, not looking at him. She was likely embarrassed but he didn't judge her for her emotions. When a person carried around such tension for too long it didn't take much for the last pebble to break them down.

"I'm sorry for my display. I would blame you, but since you were also the source of comfort, doing so seems uncharitable."

He laughed, which was what she'd clearly intended to ease the moment.

"I'll sound like a boor to admit it, but I'm glad to have been able to do both."

"You're glad to have made a woman cry? That is quite boorish."

"I'm glad to have given you the safety to alleviate your burden. Sometimes it is necessary to tear something down before rebuilding it stronger, aye?"

Only one side of her mouth raised before she nodded and answered, "Aye." Saying the Scottish word seemed to amuse her for the smile filled in completely.

"Thank you for making me cry." She took a deep breath and

began stacking pages after testing them to see if the ink was set. "I'll be out of here within the hour."

The thought of her leaving sent an unsettling chill through his body. He didn't like the idea of her out there where someone might hurt her or take advantage of her situation.

"I would like you to stay on as my guest," he admitted before his mind had told his mouth to speak.

She paused and turned back to him. This time she set her red-rimmed brown eyes on him. She tilted her head and stepped closer.

"You would allow me to pay you to stay here and finish my book?"

He nodded and crossed his arms over his chest.

"Aye. But I'll not take your money. You will pay me with something else. Something quite dear indeed."

THEA STEPPED BACK from the large Scot. Had she run all this way to be in the exact same position she'd tried to escape? It seemed like just her luck that this man would expect to be paid with her virtue.

It was all the more frustrating after he'd seemed so under-standing. And after he'd held her as she'd cried. But of course, that must have been it. She'd allowed him to hold her so close to his body.

It had felt wonderful. He was so warm and big. He smelled like sunshine, grass, and horses. And the way he'd moved his hand along her back in a slow circle seemed to release every bit of tension in her body.

But it must have riled his own interests. For now he planned to use her situation to his advantage. Well, he would be sorely disappointed.

She had continued stepping backward until she bumped into

the edge of the desk. It was an easy thing to reach back and grasp the letter opener for she knew exactly where it had been lying on the desk.

With the weapon clenched in her trembling fingers she let her arm fall to her side so he wouldn't see she was armed. She'd learned a lot about fighting as research for her books. But, until now, she'd never been forced to call the knowledge to action. She knew from her studies that surprise could be as much a weapon as the blade itself.

"I'm not interested in such an arrangement," she said sternly even though her knees were near to knocking.

"How can you be sure? I haven't even told you what it is I want."

She shook her head. "I understand, and it won't happen. Just allow me to leave. I don't want any trouble."

"Trouble?" he repeated.

She watched the man intently so she'd be ready for his attack. When he'd first arrived she'd noticed the deep blue of his eyes, and how black his hair was. Like a moonless night.

She'd thought him a handsome groom in just his shirtsleeves. His shoulders were broad, and he was bigger than normal men. How would she fight him?

Because as she was staring at him she was able to see a number of expressions cross over his face.

Confusion when she'd said the word, "trouble."

Followed by awareness and then shock.

"Good God in heaven, ye think I wish to—?" He cut himself off with a string of curses. Some in English, some in what she guessed was Gaelic. And while she didn't speak the language, she could tell they were curses. "Please. Hear me out. I don't wish for you to pay for your board with any part of your body." He shrugged. "Well, mayhap your mind. I want to read your new book. I want to be the first person to read *The Case of the Golden Feather* before it goes to the printer. And for that, I will allow you to stay here and finish your book. I'll even offer my assistance in helping you find a new home when the time comes, so your man doesn't need to come all this way to handle the transaction."

She relaxed so much the letter opener clattered to the stone floor.

He looked down at it and then back to her.

"Did you plan to stab me with that?" he asked.

"I would have done what I had to in order to protect myself."

"You're quite canny, you are," he said with a grin and Thea decided to take that as a compliment.

"Thank you."

"Do you agree to my terms?"

She bit her lip as she considered allowing him to read her book in its current state. Eventually she would go through it all again and note any errors in red ink made from Brazilwood and alum.

Why should she care if it were not perfect since he was using her situation to his own gain. Still she didn't think he would withdraw his offer if she refused.

"Very well. But know it will not be in its finished state."

He nodded. "Even better. It will be your raw thoughts on the page."

"And you'll allow me to stay here until I have the funds to purchase my own place? And help me procure it."

"Aye. Ye should know that if I'm seen buying a lady a dwelling near my castle, some might think you to be my mistress, being housed close to my estate for my needs."

She hadn't considered it, because such a thing seemed preposterous. But even still, she had no need for a pristine reputation. She never planned to wed. Any dreams she'd had of doing so had turned to dust when she'd been seventeen and her parents had died.

She'd come out of mourning the following year, planning to attend the Season, and find a husband. But her brother had already squandered her dowry and put them on the path to disaster.

"I don't care about gossip. I only wish to have privacy and safety to write my books. It is all I can hope for."

He tilted his head in that way that was already becoming common to her. He did it before he was set to ask a question.

"Why are you not already wed, Thea?"

She frowned and explained the situation, what had happened to her dowry.

"Your brother has much to answer for."

Yes, Stephen was in debt in every sense of the word. Still…

"It's true he's not been a good brother, but I don't like that he must pay for his debts with his life."

"If it makes you feel any better, Flint would not be likely to kill him straight out. It's not as if a dead man has any hope of paying down his debt. He will probably be put to working it off."

"I can't say if that makes me feel better. I'll have to let you know." There was something fitting about Stephen having to work. But she surely didn't want to know the details of what kind of work he would be made to do.

"So we have an agreement?" he asked as he moved toward the door.

"On one condition," she said, though she knew well enough she wasn't at liberty to make demands. Where else would she go?

"And that is?"

"My pages do not leave this house or my sight. If you wish to read the book, you may. But you must do it here." There was too much at stake to risk losing any bit of her work. She didn't have the luxury of time to rewrite something if it turned up missing or damaged.

While it meant having his company in her space, she couldn't chance it. Besides, she secretly hoped having to come all this way to read her scribblings might dissuade him from reading it at all.

He simply looked about the room and gave a nod.

"Very well, I will see you tomorrow, Mr. Stonecliff," he said with a wink.

Thea couldn't help but notice the way her stomach gave a

small flutter at knowing she would see him again the next day. She'd never felt such a silly thing before. Surely it didn't bode well.

◆ ❦ ◆

Chapter Six

IF SHAY RUSHED through his breakfast so he could get to the dower cottage all the sooner, no one on his staff was impertinent enough to point it out. Not the way he'd hardly chewed his food before washing it down with coffee. Or the fact he'd not bothered with a coat since he would have needed to wait for Cragen to help him into it. And he didn't want to wait.

He was only eager to get his hands on the new book and read a story directly from the mind of the author. At least, that is what he told himself.

However, as he took the steps to her door two at a time, he realized it might be too early to visit. Did she sleep late? Would he catch her just out of bed? Maybe she'd be in only her robe at the breakfast table. Would her hair be down? The golden locks rippling over her shoulders?

Not one of those thoughts had anything to do with the book.

Blast and damn.

He knocked and waited for Frannie to let him in. As was usual she ducked away without looking at him.

"Good morning, Frannie. Are you well?"

"Aye, m'lord. Miss Thea is a kind woman. I enjoy working for her. Thank ye for allowing her to stay."

"I'm glad to hear you are pleased to work for her. Is she available?" He looked toward the breakfast room, but Frannie gestured toward the drawing room.

"Yes. She is already working. The woman hardly ever takes a break. I worry her fingers will be worn down to nubs if she continues writing at such a pace."

"Do you know what she's writing?" Shay wondered if Thea had shared that information.

"Nay, m'lord. It's not my place to know."

He thought he caught a slight twitch of Frannie's lips, but he didn't dare call her out for she would likely melt into a puddle. He chose to ignore it and went into the drawing room.

Thea was inside and looked much like he'd seen her the day before. Her hair was up in the messy bun again, the smudge of ink was on her chin this morning and her gown was a light green rather than blue. Those were the only real changes Shay noted.

He wondered how she did this day after day. Sitting in the same place, fingers flying over blank pages to capture the words her mind put together in the most enticing ways. Perhaps to her it wasn't as if she were sitting in one place. As the author she was off on the same adventures as her characters.

Maybe that was why she seemed so far away.

It only took one throat clearing to gain her attention this morning. Perhaps she was not so deeply embedded in her story yet that day.

"Good morning, Lord Flemming," she greeted him with a smile and he wanted for anything to tell her to call him Shay, but of course, he could not. It wouldn't be proper.

Nor would the fact that he was in the room with her alone and planned to stay that way for the better part of the day. Still he'd not push things.

"Good morning to you as well, Thea."

"You are ready to begin reading my newest book?"

"If it is convenient for me to do so while you work. I can assure you I'm a very quiet reader."

"As you've observed already, once I'm engaged in my writing

I hardly notice much else that goes on around me."

He nodded.

"If I may, I have a few questions," he said. His questions had only been keeping him up most of the night, so he was pleased when she nodded. "How long have you been writing? The first Theodore Stonecliff novel came out near eight years ago. You would have only been nineteen."

"That's correct. I've always loved reading, and as a young girl I would often write my own stories when I had nothing new to read. They were generally tales of horses and fairies. But after my dowry was lost and there was no money for books, I turned to writing my own tales. *The Case of the Widow's Veil* had been written as I sat in my room watching life outside my window. Lady Worthington lived next door and was newly widowed. She was quite young and beautiful and her husband was an old, crochety man. I'd heard him bellowing at times."

"I'd met him and can say bellowing was his common volume."

She smiled and continued.

"A few days after the man died I was sitting at my window which looked out into their gardens and I saw Lady Worthington come out and sit on a bench near the far corner of the area. She was dressed in full black including a heavy black veil. But as she sat she peeled back the lace and removed the veil and she was smiling. Not just the smile of sitting in the sunshine on a lovely day, but this smile…"

Even knowing the details of the book she spoke of, and knowing what happened, he found himself eagerly anticipating her next words.

"That smile was the expression of a woman who was utterly joyful. I'm sure what I witnessed was merely the woman appreciating her freedom after years of being married to a tyrant. Even though I wasn't out in Society, I knew Lord Worthington arranged the marriage with Lady Worthington's father to get ownership of the land between their properties in Sussex. But my imagination set off on an alternative reason for the woman's glee."

"It is surely one thing to write for one's own entertainment and another to have a book published and sent out into the world."

The sparkle he'd noticed in her eyes as she spoke of writing seemed to dim somewhat as she looked down at her ink-stained fingers.

"Stephen went through the money at an alarming rate. He'd had a few hefty losses and the staff was let go. There was no food in the house and I began to panic. He was younger than me, yes, but as my brother and the viscount, I'd thought he would take care of me." She frowned. "That night as I lay in bed, unable to sleep for the hunger, while my brother was out yet again, I came to the awareness that what I'd always thought was not true. Stephen wasn't going to take care of me. I would have to see to things myself. I knew I needed to find a way to earn enough money to buy food, and heat our home when winter came. I first thought to take on sewing, but I had never been very proficient with a needle and thread, and it didn't make much money. As I looked around my rooms considering what I might do, my gaze fell upon the pile of papers. The manuscript for *The Case of the Widow's Veil*. And I had an idea. I knew no publisher would buy a novel written by a woman, so I planned and plotted and hired my man of business to see to the things I could not."

"Amazing."

"I didn't realize I would sell so many books or make quite so much money. And while doing something I loved. Originally, I thought only to have enough for food, but then I thought perhaps I could replace my dowry and I might somehow still have a chance at the life I had planned. But as we've already discussed, my brother suffers from a sickness. When I came to him and told him I'd found the funds in the library and wanted to use them for my dowry, he spoke of using that money to win an even larger sum so he might put everything back to rights."

"I can only imagine the money was gone that same night."

She let out a breath. "You would be correct."

"I'm sorry," he said feeling the weight of his own guilt.

"You've nothing to be sorry for. It is not your fault," she said kindly, but he knew that wasn't exactly true.

LORD FLEMMING PEPPERED Thea with more questions, and she found it was rather enjoyable to have someone to speak to about her life these last eight years. Other than the MacLains, no one knew what she'd done to survive.

Since she'd never had a proper come out, she didn't know many ladies of the *ton,* but even still she knew she would not be accepted if anyone were to find out the real reason her fingers were always stained with ink.

And now this stranger knew everything. He knew things she'd not even shared with the MacLains simply because he'd asked.

The way he'd listened without judgment gave her the courage to tell him even more of her truth until eventually Frannie came in with the noon meal and Thea realized she'd hardly finished a full page of writing.

She'd never be able to leave the man's home at this rate.

"I brought some for you as well, my lord."

Frannie handed the large man a dish with stew and a piece of bread before she set Thea's meal on the edge of the desk.

"Best eat it while it's still hot today, miss," Frannie warned.

"You take your meals at your desk instead of the dining room?" the marquess asked. Even that question had been edged only in amusement rather than judgment.

"I know it's improper, but it allows me to continue working. Besides, there is no one in my dining room to notice I am not there."

The man chuckled. "I have the same predicament in my own dining room." Carrying the dish over to the small table by the window, he nodded. "Shall we sit here and converse while we eat? Afterward you have my word I will stop my yammering and allow you to get to work."

She smiled and joined him at the table. Recalling her lessons on deportment she extended her best manners and noticed for such a large man he was very graceful and tidy as he finished every bite a few minutes before her.

"Frannie was right, it is better when it's hot." When the girl came to take their dishes, Thea noticed her smug smile but said nothing. While Thea was thankful to have someone in the house tasked with making sure Thea ate at some point during the day, the younger woman had taken on the role of being Thea's mother.

Thea didn't argue for it was nice to have someone care. It had been so long since anyone had.

She hated when she turned pitiful. She'd long since given up the habit of curling up in a ball on her bed and crying until her eyes ran dry and her throat burned. Nothing productive had come of it. Her tears certainly hadn't brought her mother back to her or improved their household situation.

For all this time she hadn't needed anyone. She'd made sure of it. Sure she required a man to turn in her manuscripts and collect her earnings, but she was able to pay for such a service rather than to depend on anyone's charity.

Definitely not Lord Flemming's.

She returned to her desk and dipped her quill in the ink to begin writing. She wasn't quite able to slip into that stasis she normally entered when her mind provided the words. The soft turning of pages from the man in the room with her kept her floating just above that other place.

It wasn't that he was a distraction, or much of one. He was just there taking up space. Shaking her head she began writing again.

"Might I ask a question," he said.

"Certainly." It wasn't as if she was writing anything yet.

"Why doesn't your hero have a real name? Everywhere he's mentioned it just says, 'Hero said,' or 'Hero did.' Surely his name isn't *Hero*."

"No, it isn't. I don't know his name yet. I don't know him well enough to have been properly introduced, I guess." It sounded mad when she explained it like that, but there was not another reason she could give that would make any sense.

"He's a real person?"

"Well, no. But he needs to feel like a real person and I will write him as I know him to be and then, eventually, his name will be revealed to me. I'll go back and fill it in later."

"I see. Is there any chance his name will be Shay Buchanan?"

"I would say little to no chance, my lord."

He chuckled and continued reading.

This time as she started writing again, she found herself smiling and as she thought of her hero, she pictured him with midnight hair and eyes the light blue of a winter's morning. Speaking of winter…

"Might I ask you a question?" she said, setting her quill aside as she stretched her aching fingers.

"Would it be horribly improper if the two of us just asked our questions as we have them, rather than having to ask first about asking? Seems more efficient that way, aye?"

She smiled and nodded.

"Very well. The snow on the mountains. How long does it linger?" She looked out the window at the white summits.

"Those out there will be capped until June. The loch nearby is icy, cold all year long as the snow melts. Freeze a man's—uh, fingers off."

She pressed her lips together knowing Lord Flemming had not intended to say "fingers."

"But not a woman's fingers?" she asked being sure to look innocently curious. She should have allowed him to cover his slip, but she enjoyed making him smile.

"Ye are a wily one." He was grinning as he shook his head and turned back to the page he was reading.

They continued on in silence once more.

"I know who did it," he proclaimed, drawing her attention from the words she was writing on the page. He'd been reading all of eighteen minutes.

"I assure you that's impossible," she said, maybe a bit smugly. She prided herself in making sure her twists were revealed at the perfect moment and that no one ever saw them coming.

"It's the groom. He's shifty."

She did her best to stifle a smile for he was indeed wrong, but she'd made the groom look shifty on purpose so one might think it was him. All the while overlooking the actual villain.

"I'm sorry to disappoint, but it's not the groom."

"You're certain? I might say it wasn't the groom if it really was the groom and I wanted to throw someone off." Another impressive tactic, but not one she'd employed this time.

"Or perhaps the groom looks suspicious on purpose, so you think it's him."

"You're a canny one, lass," he said, and she was sure it was a compliment this time.

"Thank you, my lord."

The room fell into silence and Thea found that place where the story took her away and she didn't notice anyone or anything until the room grew dark and Lord Flemming was gone.

Chapter Seven

SHE WONDERED IF he'd said goodbye before he left. She assumed he tried but she was so engrossed in her story she didn't notice or respond. How embarrassing. But then, it was probably for the best that he understood what was involved with spending time with her.

She waved the pages around, finding she was looking forward to hearing what he would have to say about her next chapter. She was quite pleased with it. And she'd intentionally made it look as if the housekeeper knew something about the missing feather. Would he suspect?

She stood and stretched, and the sound of the chair on the floor must have alerted Frannie that she'd stood. For the girl came in with a smile.

"You missed supper. Did you want me to bring you something?"

"No. I don't want to put you to any trouble. It's time for you to get some sleep. I'll be fine until morning."

She knew there would be food available. Not like those few days when she wasn't sure how she would survive after Stephen had lost everything. She didn't need to worry about that again.

"I set aside some biscuits for you from the tea tray. They should hold you over until morning," Frannie came forward and sat a small plate on Thea's desk.

"You are too kind to me, Frannie. Thank you." The lemony biscuit filled the empty place in her stomach. "Do you know what time the marquess left?"

Frannie smiled. "Just before supper. I had come in and asked if you were ready to eat and you said not yet. You said that three more times and I believe the lord gave up and went home."

"I don't blame him. I truly don't remember answering. My mind was—"

"Caught up in what you were writing," she said smugly. "I'm aware. I don't know what you are writing but it must be verra important." She paused. "I know my letters and can read, but it takes me some time."

"I'm writing a book," Thea confided in the maid. It wasn't as if no one else knew. Afterall, Lord Flemming had figured it out. She trusted Frannie. "As you can imagine, it's not something proper women do so it must remain a secret. No one can know."

"I'll not say a word of it," Frannie promised with wide eyes. Then she tilted her head. "Do you have villains in your stories, my lady?"

"Oh yes. It's hardly a good story without having someone who challenges the hero. He must win against the forces of evil after all."

"What is the villain's name in this story?" she asked. Thea didn't understand why the girl cared so much, but she explained that like her hero she didn't name the characters until the end when she felt she knew them well enough to know what they should be called.

"So you haven't a name yet?"

"Not yet."

"Is he quite dreadful? Without honor?"

"Of course, all the best villains are disreputable, are they not?"

"Then I think the villain's name for this book should be Stephen. And I would love if he got his just rewards. Mayhap if he were hanged, or no, that would be over quickly. Do you suppose he could come into contact with a crocodile? I remember hearing they were quite ferocious creatures that could rip a man limb from limb before swallowing his pieces whole." Her face took on a sinister smile as she considered the possibility.

"I imagine a crocodile would add a bit of drama to the black-guard's demise." Thea considered how she might work in a very large reptile and how she might learn enough about them to make it credible.

Frannie nodded and left Thea to devour the biscuits before going to bed.

The next morning, Thea hurried through her morning ablutions and breakfast so she might get to the drawing room all the faster. It wasn't that she had a scene racing to get out of her mind and onto the page, but her haste was due to the man who arrived a few minutes after she took her seat at her desk.

"Good morning, Miss Thea," he greeted her.

"Good morning, my lord."

He looked at her with wide eyes. "Are you with us this morning?" He looked over his shoulder. "You are speaking to me, are you not, or are you just answering blindly?"

She laughed and shook her head. "I must apologize for whatever I may have said or not said last night. I am to understand I answered Frannie, but may not have noticed when you left." Just saying it out loud made her cringe in embarrassment.

He held up his hand. "Not to worry. I am the outsider here, and have no right to judge whatever process that ends with a book on a shelf. You do what you must and I shall adapt. I'm perfectly able to go find my supper when I'm hungry. Though I do worry that you're getting enough sustenance."

"Well, I regret to admit it, but I did devour six lemon biscuits before bed last evening. However, this morning I had a hearty breakfast that I'm sure will get me through the day." She wiggled her fingers and took her seat.

Lord Flemming picked up the stack of pages on the settee and settled in. A little over an hour later the lord set down the pages and announced, "I know who did it."

"Do you?" she asked.

"It's the housekeeper," he said surely.

Thea laughed, so pleased with herself that he had fallen into her trap.

They settled into an easy routine over the next few days. Each morning he would come over to read, and each evening he would leave. Sometimes without her noticing, but occasionally he was able to catch her attention so that she could walk him to the door and see him off.

And throughout the day, he would charm her with his speculations on who had stolen the golden feather. They would sometimes share the noon meal together if she was able to pull herself from the story to do so.

That morning they'd only been seated for a few minutes when he asked his first question.

"How did you come up with the trickery with the boxing match in *The Case of the Bareknuckle Groom*? It seems like someone would need to know how to box themselves to have known such a thing."

"I do sufficient research." She shrugged.

"You've boxed?"

"I have. With Mr. MacLain and his son, Robert. Mind you they made certain not to hurt me, and complained the whole time, but I got enough information out of our bout. I also attended a number of matches to fill in the gaps needed to make it seem believable."

"It was. I think that is my favorite of your books."

She went back to her page and got no more than a few words in before he interrupted again.

"Nay. I think it's *The Case of Duke's Racehorse. That* was my favorite. I thought for certain it was the groom then too. If someday you write a book where the villain actually is the groom, I'll not be expecting it."

She chuckled at that.

"Very good. I did enjoy writing that one and spending time with the horses at the racetrack. Mr. MacLain managed to have me meet one of the riders so I could ask a few questions. And one evening Robert and I even sneaked onto the racecourse so I could ride the whole thing and envision what it would feel like flying over the hills and seeing the finish flag in the distance."

He was staring at her with a big smile on his face.

"I think that's what makes your novels so interesting. All the details make me feel as if I am doing those things as well."

"Surely you could join a race if you wished."

He gestured toward his large body. "My horses complain having to carry me about at a normal rate of speed. I can't imagine one of those light-winded, knobby-legged, Arabians having to take on such a task."

"They are far sturdier than they look."

His only answer was noise similar to a "hmm" but somehow grumpier. He went back to reading and she began scrawling again.

It was she who interrupted them next.

"I wonder, my lord, do you know anything about crocodiles?"

He smiled and nodded. "I have a book about them in my library. I will bring it for you tomorrow. But you must tell me what you plan to do."

"You'll find out soon enough," she teased.

"Canny lass," he said before he began reading again.

SHAY FROWNED AT the rain pelting the glass of the morning room as he ate his breakfast. It rather reflected his mood this morning, after he'd spent most of the night battling nightmares instead of sleeping.

The shower would not make for an enjoyable walk to the

dower cottage. He didn't mind getting wet, but being wet the rest of the day as he lounged around in Thea's drawing room was another thing.

He shook his head, wondering why he thought of it as *Thea's* drawing room when it was *his* house. Mayhap because she seemed to belong there and he had no plans to cast her out. He was enjoying her visit too much.

He'd never known how much went into the books he enjoyed. He didn't know about the research or the almost trance-like way an author slipped into their story without any notice of the outside world. At least, he assumed other authors did the same thing. But then he only knew one author and she'd surely not turned out to be who he would have expected when he read a Theodore Stonecliff novel.

"It looks like a good morning to see to the correspondence piling up in your study," Mrs. Murray said as she entered the morning room and poured him another cup of coffee.

He frowned at the thought of not being able to go to the dower cottage, but she was right. He had become derelict in his duties as marquess over the past week. It was something he'd promised the auld marquess he would never do. That he would see to his responsibilities and his tenants.

"You see to their needs and they will see to yours. It's a relationship not unlike a marriage. Not that I would know anything about marriage," Lord Flemming had said with a wink at Harrington.

Shay had never wanted to let anyone down. Even if he'd once let down the person who'd needed him most.

He went to his study and waded through the letters that had arrived. Martin had sent the accounts for *Noire* over the past month and Shay frowned. Reese was right, he should sell the business. If anyone found out he was engaging in work, he would be found even more unfit than he already was.

He didn't need to give the *ton* any more reasons to find him lacking.

It was different here in Scotland, where he was not looked

down upon for his blood. In fact, a large number of the missives that had arrived were invitations to a multitude of events being held locally.

Word spread quickly when the marquess was in residence. Unfortunately, he would have to send his excuses for he'd much rather spend his evenings talking with Thea than attending a dinner or worse yet, a ball.

But his responses would need to wait for now. Because as if the heavens knew he wasn't to be kept inside, the rain subsided and the sun came out.

He nearly ran into Mrs. Murray on his rush to leave the house.

"I've gone through all the correspondence and there's nothing that needs my immediate attention. I'll take care of it later," he explained, though he surely didn't need to explain anything to his housekeeper. Still he didn't want her to worry over him.

"Why don't you have the lady come up to the castle so you would be more comfortable," Mrs. Murray suggested.

Shay paused in the hall and considered the suggestion, but he couldn't imagine Thea would agree. Not that he didn't enjoy the thought of her sitting in his drawing room here, where he would actually fit on the settee.

Then he began to think of other scenarios that were just as unlikely to happen. Like picking her up when she fell asleep at her desk and carrying her off to his bed.

How she would wake up and smile at him, and…

He curbed that fantasy immediately.

"We are fine where we are," he said as he walked away, pressing a palm against his hardening cock. They were fine where they were, but more importantly they were safer where they were as well.

✦ ⟐ ✦

Chapter Eight

S HAY ARRIVED LATER in the morning, and Thea guessed he had waited for the rain to abate before coming down to the cottage.

"Here you are, my lady," he handed over a thick book, simply titled *Reptilians*.

"Thank you," she said with more excitement than such a book warranted, but she did enjoy learning new things.

"I can't wait to find out what you plan to do with your new knowledge about crocodiles," Lord Flemming said with a raised brow. If he expected her to tell him, he was sadly mistaken.

"It is something for Frannie, actually," Thea said with a secret smile. She hadn't decided yet if she would name the villain after her brother, but she did feel like she owed Frannie that much. "You will have to wait and see."

She handed over the stack of pages he had yet to read and watched as he settled on the small settee. Surely it couldn't be comfortable for him. She imagined a bed would be better suited for someone of his size. Then she imagined the marquess lying in her bed upstairs and was shocked by how her heart fluttered at such a vision.

Whyever would she think of him—or any man for that matter—in such a way? She had long given up on such fantasies. She was not destined to marry. She didn't want a husband. Someone who would order her about and take control over her affairs.

Besides, even if she had reconsidered the possibility, Lord Flemming was not a likely candidate as he had literally fled London to avoid any risk he might end up shackled to a prized debutante. If he had no need for some lovely young lady, with a dowry, he'd surely not be interested in an…aged oddity. Isn't that what her brother had called her?

She pressed harder, breaking the tip of her quill. She pulled her pen knife over the nub, cutting it to a sharp point once again.

"Are you well, Miss Thea? You look angry," Lord Flemming said.

"No. I'm fine. It's just this quill that is giving me grief."

He sat up. "Should I go fetch you a new one?" he offered, kindly. She wanted to think he wished to take care of her needs, but she knew he only cared so much as it hindered her finishing the book he wanted to read. And she didn't need anyone to take care of her. She was well-suited to see to her own needs.

"No, thank you. I have plenty." There let him see how much she didn't need him. She gave a satisfied nod as he took his seat again, though why she was being so irritable, she didn't know.

Shaking her head and the unwelcome thoughts from her mind, she focused on the story at hand. The words began churning away.

Shay asked a few questions, mostly speculations regarding the crocodiles, which she deftly avoided answering. Then he fell quiet for far longer than was normal. When she realized she'd gone more than an hour without interruption, she looked up to see Lord Flemming had laid out across the settee and fallen asleep.

This couldn't speak well of her book if it put the man into a slumber. She was about to rouse him to ask what page he was on so she might add in some bit of excitement at that point of the story when she stopped to look at him closer.

He was quite large. She'd thought so many times since he'd towered over her, but the way the settee failed to support his entire frame made it all the more evident now. His head rested on the arm but his legs hung over the opposite end by a little more than a foot.

And his feet were large as well. Which was a silly thought. Of course, his feet would need to be large enough to keep him from falling over. Everyone knew a tall building needed a wider base.

His shoulders didn't fit across the settee either. His arm hung out past the edge, which was probably why he had his arm bent over his flat middle. The sun was coming through the window, touching his dark hair. It didn't lighten up the strands in the slightest. Stephen's hair appeared dark until the sun hit it. Then it flared with blond and even auburn strands. But Lord Flemming's hair was only black. The deep black of her inkwell.

His hands were large. She didn't know why she continued to be surprised by how big each of his body parts were. He was a large man. If he had anything normal sized it would seem odd. There was no reason for her to continue cataloging everything separately. Still she continued noting his features as she came closer.

My, but she'd been staring at him for some time. Eventually, she nudged his arm with her hand. He started awake as if ready for battle, causing Thea to jump back and trip over the low table next to the settee.

She went over landing on her back and head with an "oof."

"Miss Thea!" he shouted and jumped up to come to her aid. "I'm sorry. I should have warned ye never to wake me. I'm uncivilized about it. Are you well? Should I call for a doctor?"

He helped her to sitting and she rubbed the back of her head where a lump was already forming.

"No. I think I'll be all right. Just a bump." She winced and pulled her hand away, glad to see there was no blood. What she wasn't expecting was for Lord Flemming to put his hands in her hair. With the gentlest of touches he removed the pins. She felt the weight disperse from the top of her head to her shoulders and down her back.

When she looked over at him she saw his blue eyes had turned darker. No. They only looked that way for the pupils had enlarged to take up most of the blue. He must surely be in a fright for such a reaction.

"Thank you, that does help some," she said.

Lord Flemming seemed to be frozen with his hand in her hair.

"Thank you," she repeated, louder this time. She managed to shake him out of the trance he'd fallen into.

"Of course," he said and pulled his hand free of her hair.

"Why did you fall asleep?" she asked, while rubbing her head again.

"What?" he asked.

"You were reading my book, but then you fell asleep which means it must be boring."

His eyes went wide.

"Nay. It wasn't boring. I just don't always sleep well so I generally fall asleep at some point throughout the day. Please don't think my dozing off proves anything about your writing."

She nodded, reluctantly. "I suffer the same ailment. Even more so, recently."

"You're worried you will be found here," he guessed correctly.

"I dream that Flint arrives and captures me. He's a large, hideous beast and I can't escape him."

Lord Flemming chuckled. "Flint is about as tall as you and is a frail old man. I'd reckon you would be able to fell him with your boxing skills."

"You've met Flint?" she said in some surprise. She thought the man to run gaming hells in the stews where proper gentleman didn't visit.

"Aye. He runs a number of gaming hells I have been known to attend."

"Oh. I see." He was gambler. Just like her brother. Which meant she would not be able to count on his help if she were to need him.

He'd offered to help her find a home, but that seemed unwise. It was better she fended for herself than to depend on a stranger. As soon as she had the money from her book, she would reach out to Mr. MacLain and have him come to Scotland to help her buy her new home and she would leave this place and Lord Flemming.

She was wrong to have thought to trust the man, or any man for that matter. She would need to do better at protecting herself. For, after all, she was the only person she could depend on.

⇶⇷

SHAY HAD DONE something wrong. It was the only explanation for Thea's sudden distance. When before they'd been sharing tales of their lack of sleep, she'd shut him down and gone back to her writing.

That was after she'd whipped her hair up into a tidy braid that hung over her left shoulder. That hair had nearly ended him. Not only was it soft and the color of gold, but it smelled of oranges and jasmine.

He shook himself again to focus on the problem at hand. Thea seemed to have gone quiet as soon as he'd admitted to knowing Flint.

He'd interrupted her more than was kind over the last few days, but she'd not seemed bothered until now. Now her hand was moving so quickly across the paper he worried he wouldn't be able to read her penmanship when it came time for him to get to that chapter.

"You know I would never tell anyone where you are?" he mentioned. If she needed reassurances about his loyalty, or his concern for her safety, he would be happy to oblige.

"So you've said."

She did not sound reassured. In fact she sounded…angry, if

her biting tone was any evidence. Rather than continue to guess at what could have caused the change in her demeanor, he just asked. He didn't spare a lot of patience for guessing what another person was thinking or feeling.

"What is wrong?" He preferred to get right to the matter. The sooner he could fix what he'd done in error.

"Nothing at all."

"Thea," he said her name like a plea. She stopped writing but didn't raise her head. He thought getting her to pause was a feat in itself.

"If you don't mind, I'd like to be alone. Perhaps you could finish your nap at the castle."

He let out a breath. Clearly she was dismissing him. He decided to give her the space she requested rather than back the kitten into the corner where he would surely feel the wrath of her claws.

"Very well. I will see you tomorrow."

The tight smile she offered him proved what a poor liar she was. She would have lost her arse at one of his tables.

He was nearly back to the castle when he realized what had riled his guest. Of course, she wouldn't think highly of anyone who spent their time at the gaming tables. Not after having her life turned upside down because of a person who couldn't manage to stop.

Thea likely thought all gamblers the same. She wouldn't have spent any time in a gaming hell to know the difference between a man who played for sport and one that played because he couldn't walk away.

Shay had seen every sort of player over the years. It all came down to how much money a man still had when they left. A casual player lost only what they planned to lose that night. Some evenings they went home that much poorer while other times they returned with more than they'd started with.

Others treated it like their very business. They played heavy but smart, and they were content to walk away when the tables weren't turned in their favor rather than lose more than they could manage.

And then there were the men like Stephen Rockledge who weren't able to stop. Not even when they ran out of coin.

To Thea, gamblers all looked like her brother. She'd taken his comment and tidily cast him in with the lot of Lord Percival without another thought. Lord only knew what she would think of him if she knew everything.

With a disgruntled sigh he went to the library and pulled out *The Case of the Duke's Racehorse*. But this time as he read, he pictured Thea riding the circuit in the dark to get the feel of the track so she might describe it correctly.

He fell asleep in the library, as was common when he was in residence. Also common was that the nightmares began as they always did. Familiar with them as he was after all these years, he knew well enough he was dreaming. It didn't stop him from feeling the fear he always felt when he walked into that stable. He felt the flask of water fall from his chilled hands. In his dreams it was difficult for him to run, when in real life it had been a quick thing to get to the other boy's side.

Shay tried to wake him, but he didn't stir, his skin had already gone cold in the winter air. But unlike all the other times he'd dreamed of that day, something did change. For this time the boy opened his eyes, looked straight into Shay's soul, and spoke.

"You're a liar," he said.

Shay woke, gasping for air with a racing heart.

In an effort to force the fear away, he scrambled for something else to think about and grasped onto what he'd been thinking about before he'd fallen asleep.

Thea had judged him because he'd admitted to attending gaming hells.

While he was in no danger of giving up his soul to the cards and dice, he understood why she was wary of such activities. She would not allow herself to become close to another man who may need her to cover his debts.

And if hearing he attended games at Flint's tables worried her, surely finding out Shay owned such an establishment himself would not win her over to trusting him again.

For now, he would need to keep it a secret.

He realized as he devised his plan that this extra heaping of secrets might account for why his dream had changed. For he did his best not to lie, save for the biggest one he had ever told, but now he would need to lie to Thea.

For some reason he couldn't explain, that didn't sit well with him.

Not at all.

Chapter Nine

AFTER FRANNIE SHOOK Thea awake the second time, Thea gave in and went upstairs to her bed. It was quite late. In fact, it was already the next day, but Thea had needed to make up for the words she lost that day because of the marquess's interruptions.

A twist of guilt gripped her when she thought of Lord Flemming. While they'd been friendly previously, she'd all but kicked him from the cottage after he'd told her he had gamed in Flint's houses.

Had Lord Flemming played against her brother and won? That last part was a given. If they'd played at all, Stephen would have lost because her brother *always* lost.

But not all men were like her brother. Just looking around her room she could see that nothing had been stripped from the cottage to cover an enormous debt. The man's clothes were well tended and the servants were happy. All signs that the Flemming estates were in good health.

Not that it was her place to judge. But that hadn't kept her from doing just that. She cursed into the darkness knowing she would need to find a way to apologize to the man in the morning when he arrived.

She'd been rude when he'd been nothing but kind. He'd

allowed her to stay on his property when he had every right to throw her out. She needed to find a way to make it up to him.

Surely there was something she could do for him.

She didn't sew or knit. Nor did she paint or sculpt. The only skill she possessed was writing and she was already busy with that. Still, she would look for some way to make herself useful.

⇛⇚

SHAY ROSE LATER than normal after a night fraught with demons and frights. He ate his breakfast quickly and was just ready to leave the house for the dowager cottage when Mr. Murray came in.

"A caller, m'lord. The Baron Whimsley."

It was all Shay could do not to outwardly shiver.

"How did he find out I was in residence?" he whispered to the butler. Though from the sheer size of invitations he'd received the day before it was clear everyone knew he'd arrived.

"From no one in this house, I can assure you. He likely peeked in the windows."

"I assume you jest, but I wouldn't put it past the man." Passing his snickering butler, Shay headed for the drawing room to find the short, toad-looking man studying a figurine purchased by some Buchanan long before he'd come to live there.

"Lord Whimsley, it is a—"

The man squeaked in surprise, dropping the figurine which shattered on the floor and cut off Shay's lie at just the right place.

"Dear me, I am so very sorry, Lord Flemming. I do hope it was not of great value."

The man surely had the funds to buy ten replacements but he was perhaps the most miserly man Shay had ever known. He would split a hay penny into a quarter if given the chance.

"Don't worry over it." Shay rang for Mrs. Murray who sent a maid in to tidy up while at the same time requesting tea be brought to the drawing room. Shay had tried to signal to the woman that he didn't need tea for that would only extend the man's visit. Truly it had already gone on long enough, and they'd yet to take their seats. Ready to move on with it, Shay sat, as did Lord Whimsley.

"I hope you didn't run into trouble in London," the man said. "You have returned before the Season is even half over."

The man rarely came to town, Shane was surprised the man even realized it was the Season.

"I had things to see to here." Like avoiding everyone but Thea Rockledge.

"Everything is so overpriced in Town. I don't blame you for returning home as soon as possible. I assume you did not return home with a wife?" He chuckled at his own joke.

"You would assume correctly." Though he could have easily found ten wives if he'd wished it, and it weren't illegal. It seemed each year the marriage mart became more desperate. Fortunately, Reese attracted more notice than Shay.

"Good for you, Flemming. I've come to invite you to a dinner we are holding in your honor tomorrow evening. To welcome you home, my lord."

"Please, you needn't make such a fuss on my account." Shay deeply wished the man would have agreed, but of course that is not how things were done in polite society. Damn it all.

"It is our pleasure to greet you properly. Say eight o'clock?" the man pushed. Shay wondered if he would need to bring his own plate of food for the expense of feeding everyone would surely be too great for Whimsley.

Since the man gave him a fair deal on hay from his own fields, Shay felt somewhat obligated to attend. Perhaps if he stayed out late enough he'd be too exhausted to dream. That would be a blessing.

"I'll be there at eight," Shay consented.

"Splendid."

Shay had hoped with the invitation accepted, that the man

would be on his way, but no. He stayed until the tea tray was delivered and set upon it like locusts on a tender crop. Not a biscuit or pastry was spared.

When he began eyeing the door as if waiting for Mrs. Murray to come in and bring more, Shay took matters into his own hands.

"Well, I should be off for my ride. I must see to some things on the property." That was true, if not vague.

"Oh, yes. We so look forward to tomorrow evening. I'm sure it will be a successful gathering."

Successful? Shay simply smiled and nodded. He didn't know how successful a dinner could be. So long as one could get the food from one's plate to one's mouth, the purpose was certainly achieved. But rather than comment, and stop progress when the man was making to leave, Shay let it drop.

Mr. Murray brought the man's hat and saw him out the door. With his guest gone, Shay made for the back door so he could see Thea. Nay. Not so he could see Thea, of course, but because he wanted to read more of her latest book.

As he walked faster, however, he knew it was because he also wanted to see the woman. Rather than lie to himself he decided to acknowledge that she was a beautiful, smart, witty woman who intrigued him. But that was all.

He was intrigued. Not interested, and definitely not smitten. Just intrigued.

He would much rather spend the following evening with her than go to Lord Whimsley's home. It had been a few years since Shay had been to the baron's house. The man had five young girls who'd not been old enough to sit for dinner, but who had entertained the guests with their singing. Though Shay had heard hounds hit more melodic notes than those girls.

Hopefully they'd improved as they'd matured.

Shay stopped walking, right there on the trail to the dowager cottage. He did a few simple mathematical calculations and guessed those squawking girls were likely between the ages of sixteen and twenty.

"Bloody hell." He thought he may have puzzled out how such a dinner might be *successful* after all. If a tone-deaf baron's daughter were betrothed to a marquess, it would surely be considered successful by Lord Whimsley.

What had Shay gotten himself into, and more importantly, how would he get himself out?"

LORD FLEMMING WAS late.

Well, not late exactly as they hadn't made any finite plans as to when he would arrive, or even if he would arrive at all. He'd said he would see Thea the next day but now here it was the next day, and near to noon, and he'd yet to arrive.

She couldn't help but worry that it was due to her rudeness the day before. She'd jumped to conclusions about him and hoped to find a way to apologize today.

If he ever came back, that is.

She hated that she couldn't seem to settle without him sprawled across the settee. She'd left that space free of drying pages specifically for him and now he wasn't even here.

She'd almost worked herself up to a frazzle, ready to head up to the castle herself and demand to know why he had not graced her with his presence, when she heard his heavy boots on her front porch. It was ridiculous that the sound made her shoulders relax and a smile pull at the corner of her mouth. Why was she smiling because a man came to read her book?

He didn't care about her. He enjoyed an intriguing tale. That was all.

He nodded when he entered the room without waiting for Frannie to open the door and escort him inside. It might have been considered rude, but it was his house after all and it wasn't as if he would catch her doing anything other than sitting in the drawing room writing. That was all she ever did.

Usually it was enough, but suddenly she wished for… more. She didn't know what she thought by *more*, but when she considered it, the only thing she seemed to want more of was time chatting with Shay.

Shay. She shouldn't even think of him as such. She would be more likely to slip up and actually use that name if she weren't careful. She wouldn't even have known what it was if not for Frannie mentioning it. Now Thea couldn't stop thinking of it.

She'd done her best to do away with any of the fanciful thoughts of the man. But now here he was with that dark hair and those warm blue eyes. At least she'd stopped noting all the ways his body was large.

"Is everything well?" she asked when he simply stood there in the drawing room looking around as if he'd lost something. Perhaps there was a more serious reason why he'd been late. Not that he was late.

"I'm not sure. I believe I've gotten myself into something sure to cause regret and possibly life-altering ramifications."

"Is there anything I can do to help?" she offered. After all, she'd wanted to find some way to show her gratitude for his letting her stay while also making up for her rudeness the day before.

He shook his head, but then stopped as he looked her over. A slow smile pulled up his mouth and she would not admit under penalty of death how the sight of it made her stomach flutter.

"Aye, Miss Rockledge, I believe there might be something you can do to help."

He let out a slow breath which caused a bit of worry to distract her from his roguish grin.

"I wonder, *Mr. Stonecliff,* do you have any need for research on pretending you're betrothed to a marquess to save him from being hunted by five baron's daughters at a country dinner tomorrow night?" He laughed nervously. "Please, Thea. I'll beg if needed. Save me."

He had actually folded his hands together in front of him.

"You act as if every young miss plans to lure you into a trap."

"I'll remind you, I am a marquess, dear lady. And, so I've been told, not a hideous one, at that."

She couldn't argue with that, but she could needle him a bit. "Not a humble one either it would seem."

He only chuckled at the words she'd muttered loud enough for him to hear.

"My coffers, while not overrunning with coin are not dusty either. And here in the country with no Season to explore one's options, desperation begins to swell."

"Hmm. While I would not mind a nice meal while watching you squirm, I did not plan for such a foray and have nothing suitable to wear." The truth was even if she'd known she would be called upon to attend a formal dinner she wouldn't have had anything proper to wear. All her best gowns had been sold long ago.

In another life she had looked forward to being invited to such events. She'd counted down the days until her come out when she would wear the finest gowns and attract a handsome man who would one day love her and be the father of her children.

She'd thought the loss of her father, sudden as it had been, was the worst thing that could have happened. She'd been grief-stricken as any daughter would be for losing her papa and then days later she'd lost her mama as well. What she didn't know then was how their deaths would impact the rest of her life.

Now she hardly recognized the girl she'd been then. And those dreams of a husband and children seemed like nothing more than a story she'd written to entertain herself.

Lord Flemming, smiled before he raised his finger and called for Frannie.

"Yes, m'lord?"

"Do you know of anyone who can serve as a proper chaperone for Miss Thea tomorrow night? Preferably not someone from

Nairnshire as we are to have dinner at the Whimsley House."

"Oh, aye! My aunt would surely do it. She lives in Inverness and she'd love a good meal and a night away from my uncle. I'll send a note straight away."

"Actually, have the carriage brought around for I must take Miss Thea into Inverness anyway to procure a gown. Might you be able to help her?"

The girl nearly trembled with glee as she nodded. "Oh, yes! It would be so much fun." Without another word she dipped a quick curtsy and rushed out of the house.

"I can't help but feel like I've been lured into a trap, myself," she said as the marquess fairly gleamed with smugness.

It seemed she was going to a proper country dinner.

Chapter Ten

S HAY DIDN'T KNOW how it was possible for him to go from utter dread to anxious anticipation for the same event in the span of only a few minutes, but he had. When at first he was desperate to find a way to avoid the dinner altogether he was now looking forward to arriving with Thea on his arm as his betrothed.

Fortunately, Lord Whimsley had only asked if Shay had married, the man had not asked if he was otherwise engaged.

After spending much of the day before in Inverness seeing to a dress for Thea and confirming Frannie's aunt would attend as a chaperone, there was not much left of the day.

Shay felt rather guilty for having disrupted Thea's writing time, but there was no rush for her to finish. He'd told her she was welcome to stay at the cottage for as long as was needed. She still seemed under pressure to get out of his way, but he rather liked having her there.

As the carriage pulled up in front of the dower cottage Shay's excitement had him opening the door before the wheels had completely stopped turning. He'd not seen the dress, instead he'd sat on a bench outside the modiste as the ladies selected the perfect gown that would not take many alterations to fit Thea. He was eager to see Thea with her hair done in some other way than a pile on the top of her head.

As he headed toward the front door, it opened and he realized her hair was only a small part of the transformation.

Her other gowns were dowdy. He hadn't thought so before, but now, seeing the way this one fit her properly he realized her other attire was likely pre-made rather than fitted for her specifically as this gown was.

The warm green gown brought out the gold in her hair and eyes. Frannie had gone to great effort with Thea's hair as it was wound in an intricate twine of braids and curls about her head with pearls tucked in here and there. She wore a simple gold locket on a black choker at her neck.

She touched it when she must have noticed him looking.

"It belonged to my mother. It's all of her jewelry that is left. I hid it so Stephen could not sell it."

He nodded sadly, hating that she had lost so much. And because of the very person who was supposed to protect her.

"Shall we?" he asked as he helped Mrs. Winters into the carriage first and then Thea. The older woman seemed excited as well, and Shay knew he couldn't show up at a genteel home with Thea alone. Even as his intended, they were not married and it wouldn't have been proper. Still, Shay wished they hadn't needed the chaperone for he had things he'd wanted to speak to her about.

"Am I to use my real name?" Thea asked.

Shay hadn't considered that she was in hiding. While it was unlikely that anyone in the Highlands would have reason to know her brother or mention having seen Thea here, the risk was low rather than nonexistent.

"What would you prefer?"

"I believe I will use my given name so not to risk not answering if someone were to speak to me. But I'll use my middle name, Sutton, as my family name. It was my mother's maiden name."

He nodded.

"This is so exciting," Mrs. Winters said. "I feel like I am part of a play."

"It would be something one might write about in a book," Shay said with a raised brow toward Thea. While Mrs. Winters knew her part as Thea's stalwart chaperone, the woman didn't know about Theodore Stonecliff.

It was not a long ride to Nairnshire, and soon Shay was reaching up to help Thea down from his carriage. She looked rather nervous and he disliked being the cause of it.

"Worry not, it is not your head on the chopping block if tonight does not go as planned, Miss Sutton."

She smiled and leaned closer. "You should not worry either, my lord, for if it were to come to it I've tucked a sharp stick into my reticule to fend off all the adoring young ladies."

He chuckled and placed his palm over her smaller, gloved hand resting on his arm.

"How did you fair with the ink?" he whispered.

"A lost cause, I'm afraid. I did my best. We'll have to say I'm diligent with my correspondence."

"You will charm them with wit, and they shall not notice."

She rolled her eyes at him which made him laugh louder than was proper. He was quite pleased with his plan to turn this night in his favor. Now if they could all play their parts for the next few hours all would be well.

⟫⟪

THE EVENING WAS not off to a great start. Even Thea, who had not been to a formal dinner since her parents were alive, could tell it was already a disaster.

They were greeted in the foyer by their confused host, Baron Whimsley. The man's smile seemed to fade as he took in Thea and then Mrs. Winters. His lips pinched into something distasteful as his brow cocked in unhappy appraisal.

But Thea nearly forgot the man was there when Shay announced proudly, "I present Miss Theadora Sutton, my betrothed."

The warmth in his eyes as he looked down at her adoringly made her breath catch. She had to quickly remind herself that it was all part of a ruse to save the marquess from being pressed into marriage by this eager father.

"Betrothed? But you said you had not married," the baron accused.

Shay tilted his head without giving the least amount of remorse.

"Betrothal is the status before one is married. Are you unaware?"

The man's face turned red and he forced a brittle smile to his face as he bowed in greeting.

"Miss Sutton, it is my great pleasure to meet you." If a person had ever sounded less sincere she had never experienced it. Except maybe all the times her brother promised her he would stop spending their money. Although she realized he had been sincere when he'd made such promises, he just wasn't able to keep them.

Lord Whimsley led them to the drawing room where six women sat waiting. The oldest was clearly the baroness, and the five younger women were the hopeful daughters who all looked at her with venom in their gazes when she was introduced.

As one, they turned toward their father accusingly as if they wanted to protest, but they had been taught well for they all turned back and gave their own greetings and congratulations.

After an awkward moment in the drawing room they were called into the dining room for supper. There was a bit of shuffling as Lady Whimsley explained she had not been expecting two more guests at her table and had a footman bring extra chairs.

As the highest-ranking member of their party, Shay was seated at the head of the table. While Thea and Mrs. Winters were directed to the other end to sit by Lord and Lady Whimsley.

Shay was flanked on both sides by the Whimsley girls who spent most of the meal fluttering their eyelashes and flirting with her fiancé. And, yes, she knew it wasn't real, but she couldn't help being put out by it.

"Are you an accomplished singer, Miss Sutton?" Lady Whimsley asked.

"Oh, my, no. I have no ear for music, playing or singing."

Lady Whimsley preened. "Our girls all play the pianoforte flawlessly, and when they sing, it is as if angels have come down to visit Earth."

Thea nearly choked on a sip of wine. That was some claim. She leaned in to look at them again and only noticed Shay.

He looked quite handsome turned out in his evening attire. And she knew how funny and charming he could be. He would make a wonderful husband to any one of the ladies fluttering around him. If he were of a mind to marry.

She wondered why he was so against the idea that he would employ such subterfuge as to pretend he was affianced to her. He'd mentioned fleeing London to get away from the marriage mart.

He must have been a man who preferred gaming and whoring to settling down. However, he'd been here nearly two weeks and as far as she'd seen he'd not once sought such entertainments.

Whether the marquess planned to marry or not was none of Thea's concern. After all, it wasn't as if he would ever marry her. It wasn't the food that tasted bitter in her mouth, but her thoughts.

Thoughts she hadn't considered in many years. Why were they coming up now? Perhaps she'd spent so much time in recent years worrying over where their next meal would come from and how to pay for the coal, that she'd had no time to recall the other things she'd once wanted.

But she didn't want those things now. She was much too practical. She wanted only peace and solitude so she might write her stories without interference. And the money she made from selling them provided the security she'd wished for all this time.

She would be happy. This was the best possible outcome. Not needing anyone. Being able to take care of herself was far preferred to having to count on someone else.

IT SEEMED, SHAY thought as he tried to eat as fast as possible, that Lord and Lady Whimsley had created the perfect sampler of women in their girls. No matter what a man's preference in a wife, he was sure to find it with one of these misses.

The youngest, Christy, was demure and innocent, with blushing cheeks and furtive glances. The next youngest, Cathryn, was somewhat of a scholar, having shared two interesting pieces of information about their cutlery already. The middle girl, Clara was flirty and funny, while Charlotte was quite serious and proper. And Cassandra, the oldest was rubbing his leg with her stockinged foot, while casting sultry looks his way.

They were all beautiful in a multitude of colorings. Some with fair hair, some dark. All with different shades of blue or green eyes. They were quite lovely.

Apparently he'd been brought there to be offered first choice from a buffet of Whimsley women, and yet all he could think was how much he would have preferred to sit next to Thea and speak with her instead.

He'd thought her intriguing for her writing, but seeing her send displeasing looks down the table at the giggling misses, he couldn't help but be intrigued by more than just her mind.

He was not so foolish to not have noticed how pretty she was in her ill-fitting gowns, with her hair a mess and smudges of ink here and there. He rather liked her better that way. But sitting at the end of the table in a new gown and her hair done up, made him think of all the dandies who would have crowded around her if she'd been granted a Season as she'd deserved.

Her life would have been so different if her parents had lived only a few years longer. And his life as well. For he'd never have had her books. And he'd never have had this time with her.

When the meal concluded and Lord Whimsley led them to the music room for entertainment, Thea sought him out and claimed his arm as would be expected of a doting fiancée.

"I do hope their singing has improved. If not, I will owe you a greater debt than I already do," he told her.

"I am much looking forward to such a concert of celestial beings," Thea answered.

"Did Lady Whimsley tell you it was as if angels had come down to visit Earth?" he guessed for it was the same thing the woman had claimed last time.

Thea nearly snorted as she nodded. "We should take our seats."

Shay led them to a place where two seats remained side by side so he could sit with the woman he'd brought rather than the other hopeful ladies. He kept her hand on his arm, and was pleased when it seemed she'd had no plan to take it back anyway.

Her chin came up slightly and he wondered if she'd been pricked by jealousy having seen him with the other women during dinner. He'd not pretend he wouldn't have felt something similar if things had been reversed. Some barbaric piece of him wanted to claim her as his own. However, he could not for he had no intentions of doing anything proper with her if he did.

Thea's life had already been difficult enough, he'd not do anything to make it even harder. And speaking of hard, having her sitting so close was making his breeches grow tight. Why did he find her so much more alluring tonight when he'd spent days with her.

Maybe it was this business of pretending they were betrothed. That she was his. Something she would never be.

The music started and Shay wondered if the atrocity coming from the instruments was due to poor tuning or lack of skill. And then all five of them began singing.

As diverse as the women were in looks and personality, so were their voices for they seemed unable to land on one melody between them. In fact, at one part he wondered if they'd diverged into different songs, for they were surely not singing the same words.

"If this is truly what Heaven sounds like, I believe I would prefer warmer climes," Thea said quietly.

Shay couldn't hold in the bark of laughter at Thea's comment. He covered his mouth hoping to hold it in as Thea patted his back compassionately and whispered to Lady Whimsley, "He's so overcome with emotion."

When Shay had recovered he leaned close to her ear.

"I don't think you need to worry, you are the Devil herself."

Thea graced him with a devious smile that had his cock stirring yet again.

Whatever was he to do with this woman? The trouble was, he knew the things he *wanted* to do with her, and wouldn't be afforded any of them.

Perhaps if she were anyone else, he might consider how to get her into his bed, but not Thea. Not when she'd been mistreated time and time again. She deserved better than that. She deserved better than him.

Chapter Eleven

THEY SURVIVED THE concert, though Thea thought it was a close thing. She didn't know if she'd ever be able to hear Piano Concerto No.2 without wincing ever again.

Eventually the night grew to a close and they were back in the carriage on their way home.

"Well, the dinner was very good," Mrs. Winters said. Even in the dark she could see Shay smiling.

"That is very good of you to speak of the things that were pleasant about the evening as opposed to mocking the musical talents of our hosts," Thea said as her lip twitched in a grin.

"I hope you're not referring to me, Miss Sutton for I remember hearing mockery coming from your lips as well," Shay defended.

"Dear me, but there is not a good thing I can think to say of their efforts except that it is over," Mrs. Winters said, casting them all into a fit of laughter.

They arrived at the cottage and Mrs. Winters was helped down first.

"I thank you for allowing me to stay the night so I might have some time with dear Frannie," the woman said. She paused and looked up at the dark sky. "It would be a lovely evening for a walk in the gardens," the woman hinted. "Ye wouldn't want to miss such an opportunity."

"Would you care for a stroll?" Lord Flemming asked while holding out his arm for her yet again. She knew what she would feel when she slipped her hand along his. Heat and hard muscles. She'd noticed it earlier in the evening when he'd escorted her to their seats in the music room.

Despite them both wearing gloves, and her being prepared, a soft breath escaped her lips when they touched. They walked on for a bit in silence but then Shay—*Lord Flemming*—spoke.

"I will ask you, as you are wordsmith, is there such a term that would mean the opposite of a chaperone, for if so, that is what I would call Mrs. Winters."

Thea laughed at his joke and then put a finger to her chin to show she was seriously contemplating his question.

"I'm not sure there's an antonym for *chaperone* but I have some words that might better serve Mrs. Winters. Instigator, meddler, troublemaker…"

"She wasn't wrong though, it is a beautiful evening. Would you care for a turn about the gardens, there was something else I wished to speak to you about."

Oh dear. She was instantly nervous. Did he want her to leave? Perhaps her presence was keeping him from the lifestyle he preferred. Maybe he didn't want to be judged by a messy spinster. She'd yet to apologize to him for her rudeness the other day.

"Very well, I would enjoy some activity after having sat about all evening."

Should she have used the word activity? What other activities could he think she was interested in? Kissing? She found she wouldn't be opposed to such a thing. Not with Shay. But that would not be proper. Still…

"I fear I upset you the other day when we spoke of Flint and I told you I'd attended games at his establishment," he said, jumping right into the delicate topic she'd been avoiding.

She shook her head.

"Please, it is I who should apologize. I have no right to judge.

I'm no one to you."

"I would like to think you a friend, Thea. And I can see how, after spending time with your brother, what I said might have caused you to think I have similar vices as Stephen. But I promise you, that is not the case. I have gambled on many occasions, as most men of the *ton*. It is something usually done for fun or comradery."

"Unless it grows like a poisonous vine squeezing the life out of a person so slowly they don't even notice." She couldn't hold in her bitterness.

"Aye. But I have not allowed that to happen and I won't. In fact, the last time I was in such a place, I only watched. I didn't even play."

She watched him closely to see if he was lying. She was always able to tell when Stephen lied to her. More recently, she only needed to hear him speak to know he was lying for it was something he did all the time. Constant promises that he was on the verge of getting them out of the situation he'd gotten them into.

Lord Flemming was either better at lying or he was telling the truth. Or it could be that the moon was not quite bright enough for her to see him clearly. Whichever the reason, her answer was still the same.

"I'm not foolish enough to think all men fall into ruin who visit a gaming establishment. Most of London would have gone to waste by now if it were so. And it is hardly fair of me to charge you for another man's crimes. I'm no one to judge you for whatever you choose to do anyway. Please except my apologies for my shrewish behavior."

He shook his head and paused their walking.

"I will not accept your apology, because it is unwarranted. You have been wounded, and a smart woman would see herself free of getting involved in such things again. I don't blame you. And if you do not yet trust me, I hope you will when you see I do not gamble when we attend a ball in three nights time."

She blinked at him. "I'm sorry, my lord, but I couldn't possibly attend. I will accept your word."

"It wouldn't do for me to show up at a ball without my fiancée."

She could no longer see his face in the shadows, but she knew well enough he was smiling.

"I have no gown."

"But the modiste has your measurements, I will send tomorrow for a gown to be sent. What color would you prefer?" he asked.

"I—I shouldn't. I have so much work to do."

"It occurred to me this evening that since you never had a proper come out that you may have never attended a ball."

"That is not true. I have."

"You've dressed in a pretty gown, danced with flock of gentleman, and drank watered down lemonade?"

"Well, not exactly."

"What did you wear?" he pressed.

"A maid's dress," she relented. "But I did have a bit of lemonade," she rushed to add.

"Thea did you attend a ball as a maid to gather research for a book?"

"Perhaps." She made to look away but his finger rested softly on her chin leading her face gently back to him. "Yes."

"Will you go to the ball with me for the sole purpose of having fun?"

"I really should finish my book…" she offered an excuse.

"I've told you, you are welcome to stay as long as needed. Besides, I would prefer you not rush. I do not want to think I'm responsible for Theordore Stonecliff putting out an inferior novel."

"Very well," she said because she found she wanted to go.

"Please don't feel pressured."

She smacked his arm. "You all but forced me into it."

He laughed. "I did not." When his laughter faded, he sighed.

"I may and I shouldn't have. I'd much rather have you on my arm because you want to be there. If you truly don't want to go, I will not accept the invitation. It's not like tonight where I was trying to keep a good relationship with the host while protecting myself from his herd of tone-deaf offspring. I care nothing for Lord and Lady Pendleton one way or the other."

He had rather backed her into a corner. She considered how she might answer as they began walking again.

"I believe I would like to go," she admitted. And then just to make sure she was standing on stable ground she added. "It will be useful to have more thorough research."

⇛⇚

SHE WAS A clever one, Shay thought as he turned to walk them back to the cottage. He'd been a right ogre to push this on her, and she'd deftly sidestepped the trap he'd so delicately set.

In truth, he'd not had any plans in going until that moment when he'd asked. He'd barely remembered which invitations he'd received and recalled Lord and Lady Pendleton had been near the top of the pile.

And it was true that it would protect their ruse to be seen by Lord and Lady Pendleton. Lady Pendleton would see that everyone in Nairnshire would know Shay was off the market. But that wasn't the real reason he'd asked.

He wouldn't allow himself to pick at his true motives.

"I will need to work diligently the next few days to make sure I don't lose any writing time," she said.

"Are you asking me to leave you alone while you write?"

"No. You are welcome to sleep on my settee if you wish." He heard rather than saw the smile as she jested.

"I thank you for your hospitality." He might have said something about it not being her settee but he wouldn't risk her mistaking his joke and thinking to leave sooner than planned. He was not so dim-witted as to say something that would jostle their fragile relationship.

When they arrived at the cottage, Shay wished he might ask to stay for a drink, but it was late and he'd prevailed on her enough the last two days and would so again for the ball.

"I wish you a good night, my lady."

"And to you as well, my lord. I hope a restful sleep finds you this evening."

He nodded a bow at her door and walked back to the castle thinking about how peaceful it was to be with her.

Despite her wishes for a good sleep, Shay woke sweating and panting from a night terror only hours later. Rather than lie there desperately grasping for sleep to return, he got up and went to the library, hoping to find a book that would offer another chance.

From the window he'd stood at weeks before when he'd noticed the plume of smoke that led him to her, he noticed a light coming from the window of the drawing room.

She was awake as well it seemed. Had she had a bad dream, or was she restless with words that needed to escape her soul through her quill?

When she explained to him how it felt, her urge to write, he wanted to tell her it sounded not so unlike the need a person feels when they lust for drink or even gambling. He didn't want her to compare her gift with her brother's weaknesses, so he'd kept the comparison to himself.

He watched the light flicker in the window and wondered what it might be like to be down there where he could walk in and ask her what she was writing. Or to steal silent glances at her while he lay on the settee. He slept so much better down there with her nearby. Better than he had in so many years. Like before, he wouldn't allow himself to consider too deeply why that may be.

It was a dangerous path indeed.

Chapter Twelve

AFTER HOURS OF lying in her bed thinking about a man she had no business thinking about, Thea gave up and went to the drawing room to write. She might as well put a sleepless night to good use. She could make up some of the time she'd lost.

Sitting at her desk with quill in hand, however, she found the words wouldn't come. Or rather the words for *The Case of the Golden Feather* wouldn't come. Instead, other words came in their place. A different story altogether.

Rather than force the words she needed—something that never seemed to work—she gave her muse its reins and pulled out a new sheet of paper. She began writing from a woman's perspective. A woman who was tempted out to the gardens by a handsome man she had an attraction to. Thea's hand picked up speed as she wrote of their witty banter and flirtations.

She told of stolen touches and heated glances. The need the woman felt to feel his kiss on her lips. Except Thea didn't know what that would feel like, only the desire to feel it.

Moving on, she focused on the things she did know. Things she'd learned that evening. The way it had felt to feel the heat of his breath on her neck when he'd laughed. The thrill of sharing a secret jest with Shay. The way they'd laughed together. The way it had felt to tuck her cool fingers against his warm arm as they walked this evening.

The couple on the page had laced their fingers together, bare palms touching. It was as if their gloves had dissolved into thin air. Something she was cautious of doing in her actual writing, but it seemed right in this tale which had grown almost mystical in nature as the words piled up on the page.

The coolness of the evening shifted seamlessly into the warmth she'd remembered of a ballroom. The man pulled the woman closer as they waltzed in a room that transformed before them. At one time it was filled with onlookers and then suddenly it was just the two of them alone in the soft, hazy, light of the chandeliers above them. And then the light dimmed to an open sky on a starry night.

The gown the woman wore changed into a gossamer night rail, similar to the one Thea was wearing now, but instead of soft cotton worn thin by years of washing, the heroine in her story wore fine silk that billowed around her as she danced. Her nipples peaked through the gauzy fabric, and Thea noticed the same had happened to her own body.

The unnamed man leaned closer to whisper in her ear. A request for a kiss. She was quick to agree. Thea shifted in her seat noticing the tingling warmth between her legs. She had felt such things before. A stirring of desire, but she was too caught up on the story to stop.

Soon the couple on the page were embroiled in a seduction Thea didn't have the words for, but wished she did. For she couldn't give the encounter the justice it deserved. She found herself wanting to know what it felt like.

Heat pooled between her legs. At her age, she'd experienced such desire before and found release at her own touch. Now though, it didn't seem enough. She wished for more. She wanted to be able to tell this story from a different perspective. One of a woman who knew what it felt like to know a man's touch.

But it was as if there was a gray void where that knowledge should be. If it had been anything else she would have found a way to research the subject completely so she could write on it thoroughly, but this…? How did one solicit research on kissing and desire?

The words slowed and finally she finished the scene with two unfulfilling words.

They kissed.

Frustrated, she gave up and went back to bed to toss and turn until dawn. After a quick breakfast, she went bleary-eyed into the drawing room and found the pages she'd written the night before.

Fanciful drivel. She tossed them aside to focus on the book she would be paid to write. When she heard the familiar thud of heavy boots on wooden porch planks, she closed her eyes, hoping to fend off the feelings of happiness and excitement at the marquess's arrival, but it was no use.

"ARE YOU WELL?" Shay asked, noticing Thea looked rather frazzled this morning. Moreso than her normal frazzle. The messy bun in her hair was askew and in danger of toppling over. The dark smudges under her eyes weren't from ink. And the smile she normally offered him each morning when he arrived was a dim replica of her regular greeting.

"I'm fine. I just didn't sleep well. Too many… ideas, fluttering about." She waved dismissively at her head, and he gathered she meant the complex eccentricities that were her amazing mind.

"Something exciting for our nameless hero, I hope."

"It was all rubbish," she snapped. Something was definitely off. They'd cleared the air the night before regarding her anxieties over his gambling. But still, he couldn't help but think she was irritated at him personally.

"Do you wish me to go? Perhaps you would like to write in peace today?"

She opened her mouth as if to agree but then closed her lips and her eyes before shaking her head.

"No. You are welcome to stay. I'm just not myself this morning, but it will pass soon enough." She mumbled something else he couldn't hear, but he didn't inquire.

She rubbed her fingers at her temples and then after shuffling a few stacks of pages together she held them out to him. He gladly took the offering and all but scurried back to the settee to dig into the next scenes of the *Golden Feather* adventure.

Without a name for the hero, Shay found it was easier to put himself into the story instead of a fictional character. Within minutes he was whisked away into the adventure, trying to find the culprit who'd stolen the golden feather.

Occasionally, he would glance up to see if Thea had improved and he would find her staring off or rubbing her forehead, but rarely did he catch her writing.

The more he looked up the further he was pulled from the story until he felt the need to address it.

"Something is obviously wrong. Won't you have out with it so it can be addressed and the obstruction can be removed from your process?"

"I believe I need to go for a walk."

Before he had the chance to offer his escort, she stood and went for the door.

"I shall return shortly."

Obviously she didn't want his company. He considered returning to the castle to allow her time and space to sort out whatever was bothering her, but he was at a particularly important part and couldn't see to putting it down. He'd not be able to think of anything else.

He flipped to the next page and then the next, completely caught up in the near-miss of the hero being caught in the study during a ball, as he was rifling through drawers looking for evidence. And then suddenly Shay turned to the next page and frowned.

Thea's writing was legible if not compact and rushed, but this was more difficult to read than the other pages. As if she'd been writing it faster than her usual speed. He thought she might have been as caught up in the action as he but as his eyes sorted through the scribbling on the paper he found himself pulled out of the tale of the golden feather and thrust into something far different.

His blue gaze, the color of a frozen lake in the Highlands, held her captive. But instead of an icy chill, she felt warm—here the word *warm* was crossed out and replaced by *molten.*

Shay read on.

Their fingers laced together, palm to palm in the same way she wanted their bodies. So close.

"Dear God," Shay whispered as his eyes scoured the page. The rest of the story continued over two pages with phrases that made him harder than he'd been in ages.

…his warm breath in her ear caused a shiver of heat to chase up her spine…

…throbbing heat ached between her legs. An ache only he could soothe…

…her peaked nipples pressed through the thin silk of her night rail…

That last one threw him, not just because of her use of the word nipple, but because a sentence ago the characters had been at a ball filled with people. Somehow they were now alone and she wasn't wearing a gown but a flimsy shift. And then…

"Mercy," he almost choked when he flipped to the back and read the next line.

…he ripped the silk from her body and she stood before him naked and washed pale in silvery moonlight…

It went on, working toward something Shay very much wanted to read. Something that had him skipping words to get to it all the faster, but then it ended with only two words.

They kissed.

"Of course they bloody kissed," he muttered out loud as he ripped through the rest of the pages looking for the finale of this story, no longer caring what happened to the sodding golden feather.

He had to know what she wrote about the couple because

while he'd imagined himself as the hero of the *Golden Feather* story, he actually thought this story was written about him and Thea.

And if so, it would mean she wanted him. He shifted to relieve the pressure on his aching cock. If Thea wanted him, he would be more than happy to comply. His randy mind did not need much encouragement to offer images of Thea and him in his bed, or out in the gardens as he ripped her shift and kissed her.

But unlike black ink on a white page, this would be real, which meant when the characters reached the pinnacle of their story it would not collude with a mere "The End." It would continue on into real life and that was not something he was capable of doing.

He could not bring Thea into his existence of deception and lies. There would be no happy ever after if he were to go down this path.

Folding the pages he tucked them into the pocket of the coat he'd tossed on a nearby chair when he'd arrived.

As he made to flee the cottage, he ran into her returning.

"Where are you going?" she asked.

"I just remembered some business I need to see to at the castle. I will see you for the ball tomorrow evening." With that he rushed away, the pages in his coat felt like they were burning him where they touched his chest.

How was he supposed to go to a ball and dance with her after reading her naked—literally—thoughts on the page he'd stolen from her? Knowing she might want to kiss him.

Was he to be the one to keep them from doing something regrettable? Because that was never a role he managed well. He had always been the instigator of their bunch. Cheering his friends on to do even worse things.

And now, as if he'd hadn't already been dealing with own misplaced desires of Thea Rockledge, he would have to somehow have the strength to deter her desires as well?

When he got to the castle, he was sweaty and out of breath.

"Gracious, what has happened?" Mrs. Murray asked as he nearly knocked her over in the corridor.

"Nothing. All is well. Just have business. In my study. Not to be disturbed," he shouted as he entered the room and shut the door, turning the key for good measure, as if locking himself in the room would keep his own disturbed visions at bay. He was a man being chased down by the hounds of hell, with no way to escape and no ability to outrun them.

And perhaps he was being a bit dramatic, but Thea's happiness hung in the balance. If she acted on her desires he would have to refuse her which would surely alter the friendship they'd formed. And if he didn't refuse…

His breeches had grown so tight there was nothing to be done but to unbutton the placket and take hold of himself. Thinking of the words she'd written brought him to climax after only a few strokes. As he cleaned himself with a handkerchief, he let his head fall to the surface of the desk.

"Good God. What am I to do?"

———— ❧ ————

Chapter Thirteen

T HEA DIDN'T KNOW what had come over the marquess. One moment he'd been lounging about on her furniture, and the next he was running out of the cottage as if there were a fire he was being called on to put out.

Though it was probably best that he'd left. She'd gotten hardly anything done. She found herself looking over at him, his blue eyes flashing side to side as he read. The way his long legs hung over the edge, one booted foot crossed over the other. So at ease. She wanted to walk over and touch him to see how he would respond.

Of course, she would never do such a thing. The man was so frightened of females and marriage he'd fabricated a fake fiancée to avoid even the hint of availability.

Alone in the drawing room she pondered why that was. She knew well enough that men in general wished to delay marriage for as long as possible so they might sow their wild oats. But eventually they turned to their duty and responsibilities and took a wife for no other reason than they needed an heir.

Shay had told her about his friend, the Duke of Granton, and it seemed the shift had already happened. Finn was married with a son and another child on the way. Thea remembered the warmth in Shay's smile as he'd told her about Willie and his antics. He clearly enjoyed being with the duke's family.

Why wouldn't he want a family for himself? She thought of how she might pose the question that he would actually answer. Not that she'd get an answer today since it seemed he had no plans to return.

Now that she thought of it he'd told her he would see her for the ball the next evening so he must not have planned to come to the cottage tomorrow either.

With a sigh, Thea picked up the page she was working on and dipped her quill in the ink. Sheamus Buchanan was a distraction she didn't need. She would be better served to forget him and just focus on finishing this book so she might move forward with her own plans.

Soon enough she was back to the mystery of who stole the golden feather and had forgotten about the marquess. Well, almost.

IT TOOK SHAY only an hour to realize he could not stay at Cawdor. He would need to return for the ball the next evening but that would give him time to get to Finn's home, if he left straight away.

A proper friend would have sent word ahead that he was coming, but Shay planned to ride as fast as any messenger could, so there would be little to no warning of his arrival anyway.

A few hours later, he was pulling up his stallion in front of *Gealach* Castle.

In the foyer, Willie came running to meet him before the butler had even taken his coat. His mother trailed behind the boy.

"Hello there, Lord Haliday," Shay greeted the little boy who laughed and reached for him. "Your Grace," he added for Lily who rolled her eyes.

"Finn is seeing to something in the village, but he should return shortly."

"Eh, I didn't come for him. You and Willie are better company," Shay joked.

"Well, then come into the drawing room. I'll send for some tea and we shall have a lovely chat," Lily said.

They talked about how much Willie had grown in the few weeks since Shay had seen him. It seemed if Shay stared at the lad long enough he should be able to see him grow.

The tea tray was empty but for a few crumbs when Finn arrived. Tilting his head to the side, Shay knew the man wondered what had brought him all this way for a visit when he'd just been there not long ago, but he was kind enough not to call Shay out in front of his wife.

Lily stood and took Willie into her arms though it seemed like too much weight for such a dainty woman. Shay knew she was more capable than many would think.

"I'm to take Willie for a walk in the garden, if you did come to see us you are welcome to join us, but if not, I imagine my husband will offer you more than tea in his study. If you were to have a need."

Finn kissed her as she passed and then bent down to ruffle Willie's white-blond hair. Shay remained. When his family was gone Finn let out a sigh and nodded.

"Very well then. Come tell me what has happened. I heard talk in the village that Lord Flemming is affianced, so I'm sure you have news."

Shay spent the next hour telling the other man what had been waiting for him when he'd arrived home from his last visit. While he left out the part about Thea being Theodore Stonecliff, he did mention she had means to purchase a home nearby.

"I always knew Percival was a bounder, but to sell his sister's virtue? Only a desperate man would do such a thing. How can I help?"

"There is nothing to be done. As I said, Thea has a plan to get herself out of this trouble. She doesn't need me, or you for that matter."

"Thea?" Finn cocked a brow. "Not Miss Thea or Miss Rockledge? You're sure this engagement is fake?"

"Very much so." But what if... He shook his head. "She understands and was kind enough to offer her help."

Finn barked out a laugh. "I doubt highly the lady offered anything. Do you forget I've known you since ye were a lad and I've been part of more than a few of your schemes?"

"Fine. I saw an opportunity and took it. But the lady accepted willingly. I didn't coerce her into it."

"The fact that she is staying on your property and could be sent away at any moment is not coercion." He lifted his brow in that very ducal way of his. Why had Shay come here?

"It's not. I would never put her in harm's way. If anything, I would prefer she would move up to the castle so I could keep better watch over her." And he could read at his leisure on a settee that actually fit his body. Perhaps when he returned he would have Mr. Murray see to it that the settee from his study was moved to the drawing room at dower cottage.

No. He should stay clear of the dower cottage altogether.

"If I cannot help in any way, might I wonder as to why you have returned so soon after your previous stay. Lily and William enjoy your visits immensely but there must be a reason for the frequency."

"You didn't say *you* enjoy my visits, Finn."

"When you are in residence, my luscious wife restricts our bed sport to our actual bed rather than more adventurous prospects, so while I enjoy your visits on occasion, you were just here."

Shay chuckled. "I'm sorry I'm an inconvenience."

"Yes, well, tell me why you're back and I'll decide if I mind the inconvenience or not."

"Worry not, old boy, I will leave in the morning. I only needed a place to go for the day."

"Has the woman run you from your own home?"

Finn wouldn't know how close to right he was.

"She muddles my head. She's smart and funny. Beautiful. But she doesn't see me as a conquest or want to trap me into marriage. Which means I am able to sit with her alone and talk about things I wouldn't talk about with another woman for fear they would see it as a bond or whatever it is women see in men they wish to marry."

"In most cases they see money or a brilliant smile. Lily saw a handsome face and a charming—"

"Know I will ask Lily when she returns," Shay interrupted and Finn huffed.

"This lass seems to have her own blunt—though you didn't say how she came about that," the duke hinted.

"Nor will I. It's not for me to say, but it isn't dishonorable, despite being maybe a bit unconventional."

"I'm intrigued, but for the sake of a speedy visit, I'll move on." He stood and went to the window smiling when he must have caught a glimpse of his family. When he waved, Shay knew he'd been correct.

"Have you never been a friend with a woman before?"

"No. Have you?"

Finn nodded. "Only once. But now she's my wife."

"That is not helping at all. I cannot marry."

"Says every rake in all of England. Yet we all eventually submit and do it. Some of us are even glad for it."

Shay knew Finn counted himself in with that small group. The ranks of men who married and found a love match. In very rare instances the reverse happened as well. Some found love and married. But Shay couldn't allow either.

"I'll never marry. I can't."

"Why is that?" Again with the ducal brow.

"I can't say."

"Seems a lot you can't do. What can you do then?"

"I can avoid her."

"Yes. Good plan. Except it doesn't work. It only makes you want to be with her more. But give it a go, I'm sure it will be different for you. Being the only man who ever thought he would never marry."

"Careful, Duke. I fear you may have reached the height of smugness."

Finn smiled. "Nay, I'm sure I could be even more smug without any danger to myself or those close to me."

Letting that comment slide, Shay broached the other reason he'd never call Thea Rockledge his wife.

"The woman doesn't wish to marry either, so you see it would not just be one person bending to arrive at the match you seem to be hoping for, but two people who would have to change their opinion in complete juxtaposition."

"My, that does seem impossible."

"Did you actually just roll your eyes? Right in front of me?"

"How can I not? You show up here the very picture of a man who is falling for a woman, and expect *me* to tell you how to keep that from happening. What do you see here that would make you think I would ever dissuade a man from falling in love and having a family?" He waved his arms around the room, but Shay knew what he meant.

"You are saying I should have ridden east to Reese instead of coming here."

"I think if you truly wanted someone to tell you this was an awful idea you would have ridden east. But you didn't. You're the only one who can answer why."

As Shay lay in one of the guest rooms at *Gealach* Castle that night, looking up at the canopy, he tried to convince himself that he'd ridden west simply because Finn was a quarter of an hour closer than Reese. Or that he didn't want to reside in a castle that was perched on the side of a cliff and could fall into the ocean at any moment, which was true and something he and Reese argued over frequently. Or it could simply be that he wanted to play with Willie. But he feared he knew the real reason he'd come here. To a home filled with love and happiness.

And that truth terrified him.

Chapter Fourteen

T HEA COULD BARELY hold still while Frannie dressed her hair for the ball.

"This is all taking so very long. I don't need to do anything special with my hair," Thea complained as Frannie set yet another jeweled pin in her hair.

"Excuse me, Miss Thea, but if you go to the ball with your hair up in one of your buns you wear when writing, people will not only know you are not really Lord Flemming's betrothed, but they'll think you belong in the kitchens scrubbing a pot. Besides, an elaborate coiffure might distract people from noticing the ink on your fingers I wasn't able to scrub clean."

Thea looked down at her hands, rubbed red with lye soap, but still marked around the nail with black ink. If that weren't bad enough, she bore a callous on her thumb from constantly using her pen knife to sharpen her quill.

"No one noticed at the dinner the other night. It is a good thing I will need to wear gloves, at least until supper."

Frannie frowned at her through the looking glass. "I daresay dinner with the Whimsleys did not have as many people looking at you. I know for sure, that at least five members of your party were focused solely on the marquess and probably didn't notice you at all."

That was true enough.

"I should just let one of the debutantes have him," Thea mumbled more to herself. Except if the marquess were to marry, Thea would likely be thrown out on her ear. No new bride would allow a strange woman to live in his dower cottage after they'd wed.

Despite her grumbling, Thea was actually somewhat excited to go. It would be a better way to research what happened at an event than the time she'd served drinks at a ball in disguise. It would be fun to dance and meet new people.

Especially if those people thought her acceptable enough to be marrying Lord Flemming rather than being the spinster sister of the most disreputable man in London. Perhaps Stephen's reputation had not claimed the lowest place, but he was certainly heading there. In any case, Thea was in no hurry for anyone to know they were related.

And then there was the matter of spending more time with Shay. That should not have come into consideration, but she did find she was looking forward to seeing him after his absence from her drawing room the past two days.

She'd learned from Frannie that the marquess had only returned home late this afternoon, though no one seemed to know where he'd gone. It was none of Thea's business, even if she wondered.

Did he have a mistress he'd gone to visit? Why should she care? She wasn't actually betrothed to the man. She didn't have a say in what he did or with whom. She shook her head hoping to also shake loose the irrational feeling of betrayal.

He was giving her the opportunity to enjoy a ball as she might have done if she'd had her come out years ago. That was all.

Mrs. Winters came in then looking even more excited than she had the other night for dinner.

"A ball! It has been ages since I've danced." She stopped and placed her palms together before her. "Don't you look beautiful? I daresay the men will cause a line to get to your dance card this evening, Miss Sutton."

"I doubt that."

"Quite right," she agreed. "They will take one look at your fiancé and be relinquished to only wishing they could dance with you."

Mrs. Winters was a balm to Thea's emaciated ego. "I'm not so sure, but I will be pleased to attend a ball and dance with whomever is willing to ask."

Thea stood even though Frannie was still attempting to attach yet another pin to her hair.

"I believe I have enough. Anymore and I'll be in danger of causing injury to my neck for having to hold up such weight."

Frannie laughed and stepped back to look her over, giving a single nod of approval. Thea thanked the girl and followed Mrs. Winters out of the house just as the carriage was coming to a stop in front of the house.

Shay stepped out and smiled as he looked her over. She did her best to ignore the way her heart rate picked up at his perusal. It didn't matter what he thought.

Except that it did. More than she wanted to admit even to herself.

"Aren't I a lucky man indeed to take such lovely women to the ball? I will be the envy of every gentleman there."

Mrs. Winters tittered at his compliment while Thea looked away with her face on fire. She could only imagine the color of her cheeks at the moment. Why did the man have to say things like that. One would think he was actually flirting with his betrothed. He played his part much too well for her sanity.

When Thea recovered, she held out her gloved hand to allow the marquess to help her into the coach after Mrs. Winters was seated. Shay sat across from them which gave him the ability to stare at her all the way to Pendleton Manor.

"Is there something on my face?" she asked, knowing there was no way Frannie would have let her out of the house with ink smudges visible.

"Nay, but I must admit I'm not sure I recognize you without a smudge somewhere upon your person."

Was it her or did his voice drop lower when he said the word "person"? Why did something silly cause a pleasant shiver to shoot up her spine. She couldn't help but think of the hero and heroine she'd written of the night she couldn't sleep. How their visit to a ball had ended.

They kissed.

Letting out a quick breath, she focused her attention out the window as they waited in a line of carriages for their turn to exit. It was easier to forget when she wasn't looking at him. But in the reflection of the glass she saw his gaze remain on her. What the devil was he looking at?

"Did you have a pleasant day?" she asked as she brushed a hand down her gown as if to remove a bit of lint that didn't exist.

"Aye. I was called away to visit *Gealach*. I had business with the Duke of Granton."

In one of their conversations he'd spoken of the duke and duchess as though they were good friends and visited each other often. And there was a little boy…

"How is Willie?" she asked.

His smile grew wider. "Very well. He surely grew another inch in the time since I saw him last. I did my best to spoil him during the short visit."

"I'm sure his parents are pleased by that, my lord."

He cast her a wicked grin in the light of the lantern outside the carriage door.

Before he could say anything, the footman opened the door and Shay stepped out of the carriage. He reached up to help her down and when their hands touched she felt a strange warmth even through both of their gloves.

It was the exact feeling she'd written about while the couple had danced in a filmy existence of soft light and desire.

They kissed.

There would be no kissing this evening. They were not the characters of the story she'd written. He was a marquess who had gone to great lengths to avoid any kind of matrimonial entanglements. And she was an aging spinster who spent nearly every waking hour with a quill in her fingers.

When the majordomo announced them, it seemed every person in the room turned to see them enter the ballroom. As they made their way deeper into the room, making their way toward their hosts, Thea picked up fragments of sentences and words.

"…his fiancée."

"…it is a shame he has been snatched up by…"

"I've certainly never heard of her."

"…most eligible bachelor has been taken by…"

Thea noticed the Whimsley girls standing off to the side practically scowling at her. She guessed to these people it did appear that Thea had come out of nowhere and snatched up the marquess. She wished she could tell them the truth and set the record straight, but she found herself enjoying the act of being Shay's betrothed. Just a little bit.

She just needed to remember it was just an act.

Shay introduced her to the Pendletons and Thea told them they had a lovely home as she was taught to do. Then Shay led her off to the dance floor with Mrs. Winters following close behind.

"Might I claim your first dance, this evening Miss Sutton?" he asked formally. She was glad he'd remembered her fake name for she was too distracted by all the people, the elaborate home, and the marquess to have paid attention.

Thea was certain he would claim her only dances, despite what Mrs. Winters had said. After all, she was a stranger and to their knowledge claimed by the highest-ranking member of their community.

Thea focused on remembering the steps to the dance. It had been many years since finishing school and those evenings her mother would play while she danced with Stephen and her father.

How fun that had been.

"You are smiling," Shay noted.

"Am I not to smile while dancing with my fiancé?"

He shook his head. "That was not a faux smile, it was real. Which means it was not done as part of our ruse."

"*Your* ruse, my lord. I am just an unwilling accomplice." She smiled so he would know she was joking.

"Tell me," he whispered by her ear in much the same way the man in her story had. And like she'd written, she felt another shiver go up her spine.

Clearing her throat, she was too distracted to deflect his question and instead, she answered.

"I was remembering the last time I'd danced. It was with my father and my brother as my mother played. We started out well enough, but at some point I stepped on someone's toes and we all dissolved into a fit of giggles. After that each time we tried again it would just make us laugh harder."

"I am sorry things did not turn out the way they were supposed to, Thea. Truly, I am. You should have had your chance to shine. And to find a man who would make you happy."

"Well, it is not your fault."

He nodded and looked away, and then was silent the rest of the dance.

When it was over, she was asked to dance by a Mr. Sullivan.

"You are the talk of the party, Miss Sutton," he said, looking rather proud of himself for having acquired a dance with the person who had roused everyone's gossip.

"I'm sure many are confused as to why someone as esteemed as the marquess would pick someone so plain to marry."

He blinked. "Plain? I don't think anyone has used that word to describe you this evening, my lady."

At first she thought he was just offering empty platitudes, but then she recalled the number of bejeweled pins with which Frannie had adorned her hair. And the dress that had arrived that morning and fit her as if it had been made for her rather than altered to fit, was of the most current fashion.

Taking in these things one would think she belonged here, at the marquess's side tonight. And in fact, if her life would have taken a different path all those years ago, she might have been engaged to a titled gentleman. Not Shay, of course, because he didn't wish to marry. She might have chosen someone like him, she thought. Someone kind and funny. And… handsome.

Someone interested in her work, rather than expecting her to sit primly with her needlepoint. She realized begrudgingly that she might have wanted someone exactly like Shay—Lord Flemming.

Looking across the dance floor she found him staring at her and when their gazes met he smiled. Her body reacted without her permission, smiling back like a besotted fool. Her breath caught and her heartbeat picked up a pace or two.

Oh, dear. She'd thought her dream had made her wish for more between them, but it was the opposite. Her dream was her subconscious telling her she was more than half gone for the man.

This wouldn't do.

$$\textbf{Chapter Fifteen}$$

T HEA WAS QUIET on the way home, and Shay didn't know if he possessed the courage to ask why. It had seemed like she'd had a good time, dancing with more men than he'd appreciated since they all thought her engaged to him.

But since he wasn't in truth he'd not complained. Even when she was not seated next to him at supper he'd simply smiled at her where she sat next to Lord Barnes. The man was much too chatty by half. And what had they been laughing at?

Shay did his best to curb his disapproval. Lord Barnes, being the third son of a viscount was certainly suitable for Thea if she wished to call off their fake engagement and seek out such a match. But he'd thought her content to write her books and spend her days answering his questions.

How selfish he was to not want more for someone who had become… such a close friend. He squeezed his fingers into a fist and released them. If she wanted Barnes, he would do all in his power to see her happy. So long as Barnes wouldn't stand in the way of her writing. Shay shouldn't have to give up his favorite author. He let out a sigh and resolved himself to giving up everything about her.

Surely Barnes wouldn't appreciate her spending every waking hour at a desk with a pen in her hand when she might be in his bed. Shay swallowed, or tried to swallow down that thought. Thea would be much too busy to write once they had children. She would be an active mother, he knew. That thought caused him to envision her playing with three small children, with black hair and blue eyes, shrieking wildly with laughter the way Willie did when Shay tossed him into the air and pretended to drop him.

"Damn it," Shay muttered.

"Did you say something, my lord?" Mrs. Winters asked.

"Nay. Just clearing my throat," he said, and it wasn't even a lie for he was unable to dislodge the large mass that had taken residence in his throat.

It shouldn't have been any surprise for Shay to uncover these deep-seated desires for a family and children to love. After being alone for so long, he'd had a family in the late Lord Flemming and Harrington. As unconventional as it was, he'd lapped up their affection like a starving boy with a bowl of warm stew, which was not so much a metaphor but a comparison.

He'd been loved by his mother as well, and had loved all of them in return as much as his guilt would allow. And when they'd died, he'd not allowed himself to risk such pain again. He didn't deserve anyone's love and he didn't want to lose anyone else.

Hearts, however, were a damn mess. They didn't always do what they were bid. And sitting there in the dark carriage, he realized how easy it would be to give into those other things. To take what Lord Barnes and Thea deserved, and what Shay did not.

He would need to tell Thea she should call off their engagement so she could explore something real with Lord Barnes. That was the right thing to do and he would do the right thing.

He was able to put off the conversation a little while longer because Mrs. Winters was in the carriage, but when they arrived at the cottage and Mrs. Winters went inside to bed, they were alone.

He sent the carriage away thinking that regardless of what

happened next he wouldn't need the coach.

She hesitated at the steps and he wanted to ask if she wished to go for a walk as they had after the dinner. A clap of thunder foretold of a pending storm and from the volume of the rumbling he guessed it would be on them momentarily. As if the heavens themselves planned to stop him from going down the wrong path.

With a stroll into the dark gardens out of the question, it left either standing there until it rained or him following her inside. Something he knew wasn't proper and didn't think she would agree to.

Though it was odd since he would spend all day in her company in the same drawing room during the day, but for whatever reason it was different now. Even he sensed the change.

"There is a fine bench on the porch," he suggested and she nodded.

He followed her slow progress up the stairs. She looked like she was climbing up to the gallows rather than spending a few extra moments alone with him. Something was wrong. Rather than ask straight out what was bothering her, he inquired on things that weren't his fault.

"Did someone say something that upset you?" There were all sorts of rumors about him, many of them true, and most of which he hoped she'd not heard. Had Lord Barnes said something untoward? He rather enjoyed the idea of having a reason to pummel the man in his handsome face.

"No." She shook her head as well as spoke, which was good because he'd hardly heard her with the thunder and how softly she'd answered.

"Did you not have fun?" he pushed a little more.

"I had the most fun. It was a lovely evening. Perfect actually."

"But..." he hinted, unable to keep poking around. He was never a very patient person.

"I would ask that we end this ruse of our betrothal," she said the words he'd been expecting, but yet he sat back with the shock. She wanted to take up with Lord Barnes. Of course, she did. He could give her all the things Shay could not.

He opened his mouth to speak. To acquiesce to her request. To give her anything she needed to find happiness, but nothing came out. Not a blasted sound.

She sat up even straighter than her already impressive posture. "I understand why you wished to tell everyone you were betrothed, but I do not want to continue with the story."

He blinked and nodded. Of course he would not be such a bounder as to force her to continue with what was just one more lie on the already large pile of deception for him.

"Did you meet someone who interested you this evening?" he asked as his body tensed, waiting for her to speak the man's name who would be the first to touch her. Shay would be happy for her, she deserved every happiness. And eventually when he could unclench his hands he would tell her how pleased he was for her.

"No. That is, there were many interesting people, and I enjoyed dancing and speaking with everyone, but not in the way you meant."

"I see," he said, but he didn't see a blasted thing. His vision flickered with relief. Yet, he didn't understand what had caused her to want to put an end to it. Their fake engagement allowed her to take part in evenings like this one. Evenings she'd claimed as perfect. So why would she want to stop?

When she remained still, looking down at her twined fingers it was all he could do to keep from taking her hands in his and begging her to tell him what was wrong.

She'd removed her gloves in the carriage and in the light coming from the window he could see the shadows on her fingertips where they were stained with ink.

Some of those stains might have happened while she'd written the story of the couple at the ball.

They kissed.

The rain began, large drops hitting the stone steps that

seemed to echo to where they sat protected under the roof. He breathed in the scent of rain as lightning flashed and thunder cracked.

"Thea, I think of you as one of my closest friends," he began with another lie. He thought of her in ways he surely didn't think of Finn or Reese. "If something has upset you, I'd like to know so I might help in some way."

She shook her head.

"It is difficult to explain. Well, not difficult as much as it is humiliating."

"Humiliating?" Now he was at a complete loss. He'd been expecting her to want something else entirely.

"I don't wish to keep pretending that we are betrothed because… Because it has stirred up hopes I thought were long dead. Silly debutante dreams of planning a wedding. People asked me when we would be married tonight and if we would wed in the chapel here at Cawdor, and while I knew it wasn't real, my mind started to envision it without my permission. I thought I was past such foolish wishes for a husband and a family. It had been impossible. And I had accepted that. Or thought I had. Now, my heart aches anew for something I've known all this time I will never have." She shook her head again. "Utterly ridiculous."

"It isn't ridiculous. It's not like you are some shriveled up harpy, Thea. You still have time to find someone who suits you." Someone who wouldn't be him. Unless… Did she want it to be him? When she pictured her wedding at the chapel here at Cawdor, was it him standing at the end of the aisle eagerly awaiting her arrival?

She let out a sigh.

"You are not the only one who is unsuited for marriage, my lord. While I don't know the reasons you avoid the institution, I have my own."

"Which are?" he pushed though it wasn't any of his business. Still, he found himself wanting to know more than anything.

"Marriage means giving up control of everything to my husband. All my finances, the income from my books, my very self would become the possession of the man I wed. I don't know that I could ever trust a man enough to turn over control of my life in that way. Not after having no control as my brother lost everything. And how would I find a husband who would allow me to continue writing? No gentleman would appreciate a wife who does nothing but sit at a desk writing all day. And I don't know what would happen if I were forced to stop."

"You'd likely be in danger of exploding from holding all those words inside," he said with a smile. He was pleased when his jest earned him a light chuckle at least.

"I must be content to write the heroes of my heart, fictional as they may be. Men who are perfect because they don't actually exist."

"I'm sorry that I caused you such pain. No more dinners, or balls, or parties. I promise."

"I don't blame you for wanting some bit of freedom to enjoy society without all the trappings. I did have fun tonight. And now I can write about the experience with more details than I had previously."

Once again his thoughts were pulled to that imaginary couple dancing at the ball, and the way it had faded into just the two of them, alone in the ballroom. Was that because she didn't have the details needed to expand the scene into a real ball? Then he remembered how abruptly the story had ended.

They kissed.

Was it because she was unable to describe the kiss in the same detail as she had the way they looked at each other. Had she never been kissed?

He studied her lips, so soft, especially the way the bottom one caught in her teeth when she was nervous or unsure about something. Thunder crashed causing her to jump and jolt him from a path they would likely regret.

He couldn't kiss her. Not when she felt vulnerable for wanting something he could not give her.

Not ever.

⬥

Chapter Sixteen

AFTER SHAY'S QUICK apology and agreement to end the farce of an engagement, he'd practically ran from her, off into the rain without looking back. She didn't think he was angry. She'd seen no sign of it in his eyes as he'd smiled at her and placed a soft kiss to her knuckles before a heartfelt goodnight.

But there had been something between them. Some heat despite the chill from the storm. Some sweetness despite the coppery scent of the rain.

They kissed.

The way his gaze had lingered on her lips, she thought he might kiss her and she wanted it. Not for research, and not because she expected Shay to give way to his plans of bachelorhood, but because she just wanted to enjoy such pleasure and she'd only wanted to enjoy it with him.

She shook her head and shifted to her other side in the bed. And then back.

Thea found herself in much the same state as she had nights ago, when she couldn't sleep for thinking of things that weren't to be. As before, she gave up and went to the drawing room to find her scene of the couple in the ballroom. She had details she could add now.

Not about the ball, for she preferred it the way it was with just the two of them alone. But now she could add what it felt like when a man stared intently at a woman's lips with need in his eyes. She didn't think she had misread Shay's desire to kiss her this evening.

She would have welcomed it without hesitation.

But he hadn't kissed her, instead he'd cleared his throat, stood, and wished her a goodnight before rushing off into the rain. She'd not even had the chance to offer that he wait out the storm inside. He'd fled. That was the only way to describe it.

"Where is it?" Thea picked up another stack of paper and flipped through them looking for the story from the other night. She knew the two pages would stand out from the rest because she'd not attempted to keep her writing restricted in size as she did normally to conserve paper. She hadn't been thinking of the cost of paper at all when she'd written her steamy tale.

Another stack and another, and then she looked toward the empty hearth. Perhaps she'd tossed it in the fire with the rest of her wasted pages. It looked as if Frannie had lit it at some point for it was nothing but ashes. Even on warm days, Frannie would light a fire occasionally to help dry Thea's pages faster.

Thea felt a great loss that the pages were gone. She debated whether or not to try to recreate the story, but decided against it. There was no use. One thing she'd realized this evening was that wanting something—even something she hadn't realized she still wished for—didn't mean it would ever come to fruition.

Writing such a story, while freeing in the moment, wouldn't get her any closer to the independence she required. So rather than spend any more time on a story that had no hope of coming true she pulled out a blank page and picked up where she was with *The Case of the Golden Feather*.

She hoped much of this story didn't come to fruition either, specifically the part about the murder, but this book would be for everyone, while that other story had been for her alone.

They kissed…

She shook her head. No, they never would.

SHAY FOLDED UP the two pages and tucked them away in the table next to his bed where they were sure to be safe from his valet. He'd read it a few times that evening. The last time while he managed himself with the other hand, thinking of the couple in the story as himself with Thea. He'd mentally added on a few scenes her story was lacking which had him finish himself with a groan.

He shouldn't have taken it. At the time, he liked to think he'd done it so she wouldn't be embarrassed to know he had read it, or even so that no one else could read something so personal to her. Though that excuse lacked reason for the only other person in the cottage was Frannie and while she knew her letters and could read, she would not dare be so disrespectful to Thea.

Not like him.

He considered how he might sneak it back to the cottage and tuck it into a pile of her pages, but cast that option aside when he remembered how tattered the papers had become from his folding and unfolding them so often over the last few days. How could he explain such a thing?

Rather than have to face her after their awkward parting the night before and his guilt of using her story in such a foul way, he stayed at the castle that morning after breaking his fast. He spent the earlier part of the day standing by the window looking down at the dower cottage.

"Oh, my lord. I didn't realize you were in here. I was about to take care of the dusting." Mrs. Murray paused and tilted her head to the side. "Why are ye here instead of the cottage?" She glanced toward the window.

"I don't need to explain myself to my servants."

Of course there was no apology from the woman. She simply cocked a brow at him. "I'll pretend you did not just snap at me, my lord, for you were raised better than that."

A new wave of guilt washed over him. It seemed he couldn't do right by any of the women in his life at the moment.

"I'm not the marrying type," he decided to answer instead.

"Aye. So I've heard many times. Unless you've done something to compromise the lady, I don't see as why that matters."

"It matters because she does want to marry and doesn't think she ever will. And when I'm with her I find myself wanting to do anything to make her happy, so you see the danger."

Mrs. Murray pressed her lips into a line in an attempt to keep from smiling. After a few seconds she gave up.

"Do ye worry you'll propose to the woman by accident?"

"We're in Scotland, where it's much too easy to be married. I'm sure accidents have happened."

"I see. I shall have a noon meal prepared here and I'll see to the dusting another time. Unless you're off on your accidental honeymoon by then."

When his insolent housekeeper left him alone again, Shay went back to looking down at the cottage. He pictured Thea the way he knew he'd find her if he went down there. With her hair in a messy bun and ink smudges on her beautiful face. How long would he stand there before she noticed him?

Then he thought to a day when she wouldn't be living in his cottage. When she would move on. She planned to buy her own home, but perhaps now that her dreams for a family were reawakened she might look to find a husband. Someone she could trust with her secret.

He tried to think of her with a husband and children and felt that same discomfort in his chest. One that made him hurry for the door. He didn't slow until he was knocking at the cottage door and Frannie had let him in.

"Ah, my lord. I was beginning to worry something had happened to you on your travels down from the castle."

"Nay, I was delayed with other things." He was glad Frannie wouldn't think to question him as to what he'd been doing the way Mrs. Murray would have. Frannie was content to show him into the drawing room where Shay found Thea exactly as he'd pictured her.

Today's smudge was on the side of her perfect chin and he found himself smiling to see it. To see her.

"You will need to pick up your pace, my lord. I am quite ahead of you again," she said without looking up. "I have been at it since early this morning."

The way she shook her head made him think she was too embarrassed to tell him exactly how early she had started. He wouldn't pressure her into saying. He simply took a pile of dried pages and settled in his place on the settee.

This was where he belonged. This felt... right.

THEA HAD DONE her best not to meet Shay's eyes when he'd arrived. She'd spent most of the morning worrying over whether he'd not come because he was angry she had put an end to their false engagement. While she'd also been glad he had not come that morning so she might get control of her silly emotions for the man.

Now that he was lying out on her settee once again, she tried for anything to put all the pieces back where they had been before her desires had grown to such huge proportions. If they could just go back to how they'd been before all this confusion of her senses.

Oh, how she wished he would ask her a question about the story so they might be set back on the proper path of friendship. But instead, he simply moved page by page through the story. She knew he'd read approximately eight pages so far, for she'd yet to pick up her quill and do anything other than stare at the man.

Minutes later Frannie entered with a tray for their noon meal.

"Oh, good. I was near to starving," Shay said as he practically hopped up to set upon the food. Looking over his large form she knew Lord Flemming was not in danger of such a thing.

Thea was not hungry, but she grasped onto the distraction of fixing a plate with meat cheese and bread. They had hardly spoken and it was growing tedious. She looked over to see the marquess stacking the meat and cheese on top a slice of bread and then rolling it in on itself before shoving the end in his mouth. She'd seen sandwiches served at meals. Small triangles of bread and beef eaten with a fork and knife, but this...

"Whatever are you doing?" she asked.

He finished chewing before smiling and holding up the part he hadn't eaten for her inspection.

"When I was a boy on the streets, we didn't have cutlery. If we were lucky enough to get bread, meat, and cheese, we divided it out amongst us. We'd hold the slice of bread in our hands and then pass around the meat and cheese or what else we had on top. We were generally so hungry the food didn't last long. It was easier to roll it up to shove it all in our mouths at once. All the flavors mixing together are the perfect treat. You should try it," he suggested.

"My mother would surely come up from her grave to see me eating with my hands."

"Come now, Thea. We are in Scotland. Be a little barbaric. Call it research."

She laughed and layered the food the way he had, with some pointers from him to keep everything within the confines of the bread. She smiled as she began rolling everything together and then held it, deciding if she could really just put it in her mouth to take a bite.

Shay's roll was near to gone so she opened her mouth and shoved the end in. Tearing through the clump with her teeth gave some deep form of satisfaction. As he'd said, the flavors combined and became their own new flavor.

"Oh, that is well done," she said with her mouth still full. If she were going to embrace her barbarianism, she might as well go all the way.

She expected he would be delighted and looked up at him. The first time she'd met his gaze all day. But he wasn't laughing or even smiling. He was staring at her lips again as she chewed.

Surely he didn't plan to kiss her when her mouth was full.

But then he lifted his hand slowly, and touched the edge of her bottom lip. The contact made the sensitive skin zing with warmth.

She blinked owlishly up at him and leaned in closer.

"A bit of cheese," he explained. When he blinked, the connection was cut and she pulled back.

A bit of cheese. She'd thought the man was about to kiss her and here it had only been hygienic. She couldn't help but laugh at herself. How ridiculous she'd become. Lord Flemming was not going to kiss her.

She thought about it as they finished their uncivilized meal. Perhaps if she were to kiss him, the mystery would be solved and they could go back to the way things had been before. Thea was curious by nature and enjoyed learning new things. Maybe it was that gray void in her story that had precipitated all of this thinking of kissing the marquess.

Shaking her head, she stretched her fingers and picked up the quill to write. Soon enough she was pulled back into the mystery and solving the case. She'd introduced Frannie's crocodile, smiling when she knew how it would eventually fit into the gruesome ending for the villain.

Unfortunately, she wouldn't be able to name the villain after her brother for the thief was actually a woman. Something she had never done before and knew her readers would not see it coming.

As she wrote, she came up with an interesting twist, but one she wasn't certain would work. Mostly because she didn't have the information needed. The same information she'd been contemplating earlier.

Specifically, about kissing. Perhaps now was her chance.

❦

Chapter Seventeen

S HAY WAS ON the edge of wakefulness and an enjoyable nap when Thea startled him awake.

"Have you kissed a lot of women?"

For a moment Shay thought he'd conjured the question, but when he looked over at the desk, Thea was waiting expectantly for an answer.

Shay set down the pages in his hand, deciding how he might answer.

"Pardon?" he asked, though he'd heard her question clear enough. He only wished to give himself some extra time to consider his answer.

"How many women have you kissed?" she rephrased the question making it even more specific.

"I can't say I know the number exactly," he tried to be vague but the way her brows raised made it clear he'd answered incorrectly.

"So many you can't recall the number?" she said, shocked.

Yes. Though none of them were you, he thought to himself glad he hadn't said that out loud.

"I would say several." *Dozen.* "Is there a reason you're asking?"

"I wonder if a man can tell the difference between one woman and the next by her kiss? In this book, I planned for the hero to kiss the wrong woman in a darkened room and realize he'd kissed the person he and the heroine were chasing."

"So the person who stole the golden feather is a woman?" he asked.

She waved a hand. "She may work for the man behind it. You don't know yet." He sometimes wondered if *she* even knew yet. "So can you?"

"Can I?" He always felt a few steps behind when he spoke with her about her stories. She jumped around from topic to topic so quickly. It was enthralling, intriguing. It was… Thea.

"Can you tell the difference from one woman's kiss and another?" she asked with a slight bit of peevishness he enjoyed as well.

"Oh. Aye, I would say they are different. Likely similar to kissing men, each have their own set of skills they employ."

Thea's cheeks heated and she looked away. "Thank you, for answering. That is all."

But it wasn't all.

"Thea?"

"Hmm?" she said not looking at him.

"Have you kissed more than one man?"

She was not a young debutante. At her age, she may no longer be considered marriageable by the *ton's* ridiculous standards, but at least it would afford her the opportunity to explore something as innocent as kissing.

As usual, Shay found himself wondering as to who she might have kissed. He didn't know who this man may be, but he wanted to find him and give him a firm shaking for not marrying her to save her the fate of her brother's plans.

"No," she answered quickly. But the way she kept her gaze on the page rather than look at him made him think he'd asked the wrong question.

"How many men have you kissed?"

"I just answered you. Less than two."

"So you've kissed one man?" Did her head just bow even lower? Soon her forehead would be resting on the paper. "Less than one man?"

She nodded just once, confirming his suspicions. It was a crime that this woman had never been kissed. Before he had a chance to say so she seemed to erupt with excuses.

"I never had a come out. My brother's friends are all louts, so I'd never consider kissing any of them. The only other men I am in any contact with are Mr. MacLain, a happily married man, and…" She waved a hand in his direction. *Him.*

He couldn't help but smile. For she'd clearly thought of kissing him if she'd curated such a list of men in proximity for kissing.

He recalled the shorter story he couldn't stop reading each night when he was alone in his room. This explained the abrupt ending he'd wondered about.

He stood and came closer to where she sat at the desk.

"Thea, should we kiss for the sake of research? Even if I answer your question about whether or not I could tell one woman from the next, you won't be able to describe the kiss unless you've tried it yourself. Like boxing and horse racing." It was practically criminal the way he'd grasped onto this excuse to be allowed to kiss her without attaching any of the emotions to the act. But he was not above doing disreputable things for the sake of survival. He'd stolen so he could eat.

Perhaps this was not the same thing at all, but at the moment he felt like kissing Thea was crucial for his survival.

"For research only?" she asked quietly when he'd expected her to turn him down cold. She was considering it. He took a step closer, eager to persuade her, when he knew as a gentleman he should do the opposite.

"I would be pleased to assist you. To make the book more believable, of course."

She stood and stepped out from behind her desk.

"Yes. I think it is necessary. So that I might continue on." She cleared her throat before adding. "With the story." She stepped closer still and looked up at him.

He'd cataloged all the many colors of brown in her eyes when he'd seen them from a distance, but this close, they were stunning. So much gold and amber sparkling in the dark warmth.

"Very well, then, I shall kiss you now," he said formally as a final warning. But Thea didn't back away from the challenge. There was nothing to do but lower his head and press his lips to hers in the way he'd been dreaming of for longer than he cared to admit.

⤛⤜

THEA THOUGHT IT normal to close one's eyes when kissing. She may not have kissed anyone, but she'd seen it done and both times the couple closed their eyes.

But she found as Shay grew closer she didn't want to cut off such a vision. Seeing him so close was indeed a treat. The blue in his eyes, normally sparkling like the surface of an icy pond, grew darker.

And then, when his lips touched hers, she couldn't keep her eyes closed any longer. She seemed to melt into the kiss, allowing just the sense of heat and touch between them.

It started out as just a firm press of his lips—softer than she'd expected—against hers. But then he'd moved them and placed them again and again. Each time they reconnected, the flames in her body rose higher.

She gasped at the sensation and when her lips parted, Shay invaded her mouth with his tongue. She'd never expected this, but it felt as if tongues were invented for this purpose alone and tasting things and speaking were added on later.

Her thinking was confirmed when her own tongue as if on some instinct reached out to stroke enticingly against his. Later she might write about how fascinating the feeling was. Not in the book of the golden feather of course, but in a story just for her. So she might revisit it and remember every detail. But at the moment her mind was a muddle of feeling everything at once.

Eventually he pulled away, his breath heavy against her damp, swollen lips. She realized her own breathing was not normal either and wondered at why it would have sped up when they'd not moved.

She blinked realizing the sunlight was still coming through the windows when she'd expected it to be night with the hazy glow of chandeliers above them.

But this was not her story. This was real.

She had just kissed Lord Flemming. No, she had just kissed Shay.

He blinked and then smiled. When she planned to move her lips into an answering smile she found they were already pulled up of their own accord.

"I'm afraid there was a flaw to our research," she said.

"What is that?" he asked, still so close she felt his breath as he spoke.

"I now have some idea what kissing is like with one man, but no way to experiment with another."

His brows came together in what she could only describe as a proprietary sneer before it faded back into a smile.

"I might kiss you again with a different technique. Perhaps a few different techniques so you might know what modifications exist." He was suggesting they continue kissing.

"Yes, please," she all but begged.

SHAY FIRST BELIEVED the overwhelming pleasure he felt when kissing Thea had been because of the illicit nature of it. Afterall, didn't things feel better when they were forbidden?

But when she gave him permission to kiss her again and again, he had to acknowledge it was something else.

They fit together perfectly. His lips seemed to be made for hers, and their tongues meant to find each other. To properly show her all the many facets of kissing he'd allowed his hands to rest lightly at her hips, but this time he slowly moved his palms back and slightly lower so he might pull her closer to his body where he needed her.

When that kiss melted into the next and the next he wanted to drape her back over her desk to trail kisses down her throat and into her gown. Instead, he pulled back, giving them another moment to catch their breath.

"I'm not sure I detected a difference in that kiss from the first except maybe in the depth of your tongue."

He laughed at her innocent evaluation. Most likely she hadn't noticed a difference because he'd not changed the technique at all. He'd simply kissed her again in the way that was most appealing to him. In fact, he'd forgotten about the research entirely.

"You didn't notice the slight twirl to my tongue that time?" he grasped onto something that might have been minorly different. "Shall we try again?"

"Yes," she said, breathlessly and reached up for him. This time he allowed her to control the kiss and enjoyed the way her fingers played with the longer hair along his neck. When he pulled her closer yet again, her fingers clenched tighter causing a delicious sting across his scalp.

He gripped her arse tighter, knowing if he weren't careful he might cause marks on her skin, but finding the idea appealing rather than appalling. He'd never marked a lover in the past, but he'd never wanted any other woman to be his in the way he wished to claim Thea.

She gasped again and he pulled away, even taking a step back to make sure he didn't reach for her again.

"I'm sorry," he said. "I don't know that I'm doing a fair job of displaying the multitude of characteristics involved in kissing."

She looked up at him with a dazed expression and smiled

with lips swollen and red from his kisses. "Should we try again?" she asked.

With a growl he nodded. "Aye. I believe we should."

Chapter Eighteen

THEA TOUCHED HER lips as she remembered kissing Shay in front of this very desk. It hadn't been until they'd heard Frannie's footsteps coming closer that Shay had pulled away and went back to his seat leaving her standing there, just as the girl had entered.

Thea was grateful for his fortitude, for if it had been up to her they wouldn't have stopped in time, and would have been surely caught. Perhaps it was all the potential catastrophes in ballrooms, where Lord Flemming was nearly compromised that had made him more attuned to avoiding such entanglements. But now, days later, she felt the old frustrations return.

In the week since they'd kissed, Shay had fled her drawing room for the castle and not returned. She should have had stacks and stacks of pages waiting for him, but since she'd spent long hours staring out the window at the castle, thinking of their kisses, she'd managed only three additions and even they were likely to be thrown into the fire.

She rubbed her forehead trying to decide what to do. It was obvious to her, that Lord Flemming greatly regretted what they'd done. And it was completely her fault it had happened. She'd been the one curious about kissing. She'd been more than happy to jump to his offer of research.

She also remembered some portion of the kissing had been precipitated by *her*. Had she really grabbed him around the neck and pulled him down to her waiting lips? She had.

A groan of misery escaped her lips and Frannie came in.

"Are you not feeling well today, miss? I've heard you making noises of complaint the last week, but not as often as today. Is whatever ailing you grown worse? Should I fetch the doctor?"

"I assure you I am physically well." Though she did think she might be sick when she recalled her hoydenish display with the marquess.

"Perhaps some tea would help."

Thea nodded, even as she knew tea would not help. She thought perhaps the only thing that might truly help would be to leave Cawdor and Nairnshire. When once she'd thought the village the perfect place for her to call home, she now thought it was not far enough away from Shay Buchanan. Perhaps all of Scotland and England would be too close. Maybe she should leave for the continent.

She needed to decide and just go. She didn't know how long she had before Shay showed up and asked her to leave his home. She could only think the reason he'd not done so already was because the poor man was worried she might attack him yet again.

If she could just stop thinking of him and finish the book. Frannie came in with the tea then and Thea latched onto yet another distraction. But when the tray had been ravaged, Thea sighed, for it surely hadn't helped at all.

IN THE LAST week, Shay moved from room to room in the castle noting how much each place lacked the very thing he truly wanted. He'd start his day in the breakfast room, eating alone, and then went off to his study where he reviewed the ledgers that didn't require daily upkeep, and therefore needed no review.

In the afternoons he'd often end up in the library where he would divide his time between lying on a chaise while reading a Stonecliff novel, and standing by the window staring down at the dower cottage wondering what Thea was doing.

It wasn't an even split, mind you, as only a few minutes were actually spent reading. He'd often take his noon meal in the library and hope to be lulled to sleep, but his naps had been overtaken by more time spent in thought of Thea.

Eventually, Mrs. Murray would come to tell him supper was ready and he would eat his meal, alone as always, before he would watch the clock until it displayed an hour not too hideously early for sleep, where he would ready for bed only to dream of Thea and the kisses they'd shared.

He'd not realized how lonely his life was until he'd removed himself from the person who had become a very large part of it. What had he done before he'd known her? Surely he must have been content. He'd not remembered it being this agonizingly dull.

In those times of thought, as he was doing today in his study, he vacillated between thinking he was a hero for taking on such a herculean effort as avoiding his deepest temptation, and thinking himself a coward for the exact same reason.

Surely Thea must think he avoided her because he regretted their kisses and that was something entirely untrue. In fact, he only wanted to kiss her more, which was why he needed to keep his distance.

For kissing was a slippery slope and he feared he was not strong enough to keep himself from falling.

When the door opened, he hoped Mrs. Murray was coming to tell him it was noon, but the clock on the mantle only showed a quarter ten.

"M'lord, we've a problem," Mrs. Murray said as she bustled into his study, wringing her hands. It was rare to see the woman so upset.

"What has happened? Lady Thea…?"

Anna winced and came closer, dropping her voice.

"John just put Lord Percival and Lord Billings in the morning room. He's come for his sister. To return to London with him."

"He knows she's here?"

"He says he has it on good authority she is here, for whatever that means."

"Good God," Shay muttered as he jumped up from his desk. He worried for the MacLains if Stephen had hurt them in any way, Thea would be horrified. "I must move her somewhere safe."

"Aye. That's why John put them in the morning room. So ye might sneak out the back and ride to the cottage without being seen."

"The man is brilliant."

"It was my idea," she complained.

"Then you are the brilliant one, he is only to be praised for listening to you." Shay grabbed up his coat and tugged it on. "You keep them busy until I return."

"Aye. I plan to tell them you are out for a ride, which will be the truth as Gordy is bringing your horse around now. Go. Save her from the fate her lout of a brother has planned for the lass."

With a nod, Shay rushed from the room. As Mrs. Murray had said, Gordy was just bringing Phantom to the back of the house as Shay exited through the servants' doors.

"Thank ye, Gordy." Shay mounted and nudged his horse into action the quicker to get to Thea. As he rode, he tried to think of someplace she could go that her brother would not find her.

She'd wanted to buy a home close by, but that wouldn't work now. Not when her brother knew she'd come here. And where could she go with no horse? It would take her some time to hire a carriage for a long ride. And she didn't have extra time.

By the time he dismounted and ran into the house he'd considered and disregarded at least a dozen possible escape routes. Stepping into her drawing room he expected to see her quill scrawling across the pages, but her head was resting on her arm and her eyes were closed.

"She worked late into the night and fell asleep there. I didn't have the heart to wake her," Frannie said quietly by his side. "She's not been feeling well."

"What is wrong with her?" he asked.

"I'm not sure. She only says she's physically well, for whatever that means."

Shay thought he knew well enough what she meant. That in body she was fine, but in heart she ached. Just as he did.

"Well, she must wake now. Her brother has come for her."

Frannie gasped and he realized his mistake. In addition to his vile plans for his sister, Stephen Rockledge had ruined Frannie when he'd come to stay the year before. He'd wooed the lass into thinking he loved her only to get what he wanted and then left the girl.

Shay felt responsible for having such a monster as a guest, though he'd not been a guest as much as a leech for the two months he'd stayed on at Cawdor.

"I'll not allow anyone to hurt ye, Frannie. If you need to go home to the village until he's gone, I will see to Miss Thea. I fear she will need to leave anyway. Go on," he said and the girl hurried out of the room.

"What's wrong?" Thea asked, her sleepy eyes blinking owlishly.

There was no time to settle the news lightly.

"Your brother has arrived at the castle. He knows you're here and has come to take you back to London."

She looked around at the piles of paper on the desk, tables, and even on the settee. It would take her some time to pack her things.

"You need to leave, immediately," he said. "Don't worry. I'll pack up your things and send them on to you wherever you go."

"That's just it, I don't know where to go. The fact that Stephen knows I'm here means he's likely compromised Mr.

MacLain. No doubt he threatened the man in some way. I'll not be able to have him send me any funds from my accounts, let alone help me purchase a home. And I haven't the funds yet, because I've not been able to finish…"

Her shoulders slumped as her skin went pale. He wanted to go to her, pull her close and tell her everything would be all right, but he'd not lie to her.

"I'll give you the money. My horse is outside. You can ride to the next village and rent a room until I send the lout back to London and come for you." It was the best plan he'd come up with, but it was Shay who wasn't certain it would work. Stephen was desperate and desperate people rarely gave up when they had a way out of their predicament. Sending Thea away alone meant Shay wouldn't be able to protect her when Stephen found her.

Thea shook her head. "I can't keep running from him and putting other people in danger." She glanced over at the door where they heard Frannie in the other room.

After letting out a deep breath, Thea stood taller. "Please burn all the pages when I'm gone. If I must face such a grim fate, at least I don't want my brother to attempt to finish the book to get the money. At least my name will remain unsullied." She shrugged. "Well, the name I used anyway."

"No." He shook his head. He may have failed to come up with a good plan thus far, but at least it was better than giving up completely. He needed to save her. But if he refused to give her up to Stephen now, he would only return with the constable and Shay would be forced to turn her over to the rotter because Stephen was her guardian.

Unless…

An idea came to him. One so absurd it might just work.

Chapter Nineteen

T HEA FEARED SHE might be sick. She'd been so close. Just a few more chapters and she would have finished the book. She could have turned it in and gotten the funds needed to purchase a home far away from her brother.

But he was here. God only knows what he'd done to the MacLains for them to have told Stephen where she was. She didn't blame them. Thea had put them in a fair amount of danger by keeping her secrets.

And now Shay was embroiled in her mess. She heard Frannie upstairs packing her things and felt another twist of shame in her stomach. She'd brought Stephen here. The man who had hurt Frannie.

There was no escaping this without others getting hurt. She'd had a wonderful time here. Memories she would hold onto when her new life was not as kind.

"I'll go," she said as she headed for the door, ready to face her fate even if her knees trembled so badly she wasn't sure how she might walk all the way up to the castle.

"Wait," Shay said quietly, his hand had come out to grip her arm lightly. The heat from his hand seeped through the fabric of her sleeve and caused Thea to shiver. The memories with him were the sweetest and her eyes stung for having to give up even a minute longer with him.

"I thank you for your hospitality, Lord Flemming, but I'll not cause you or your household any more trouble than I already have. I was wrong to have come here and to have brought this risk to your home. I am so very sorry."

She turned to go, but Shay was still holding her.

"There is another way," he said, his voice still eerily quiet.

She shook her head. "I can't run far enough or fast enough. He will find me."

Shay's grip eased enough for his hand to slide down her arm and take her hand in his.

"Then don't run. Stay here. With me."

Again she shook her head. "He will only get the law to force me to go with him."

"He couldn't force ye to leave if you were my wife," Shay said.

Thea blinked as the words penetrated her foggy brain. She felt a step behind, having just woken, but this… no, this didn't make any sense.

"Wife?"

"My horse is outside. We will ride to the village and be married within the hour. As my marchioness he will not have the legal right to take ye anywhere. You would be safe."

"But you said you didn't wish to marry."

"I said I wouldn't marry, not that I didn't wish to."

She didn't see what the distinction was. Either way he didn't plan to marry.

"But I will marry you, Thea, to keep ye safe from being given over to a man like Flint. Let me protect ye, lass. Please."

"To agree would be such a selfish thing. Cursing you to a life with me when you might meet someone you truly want, just to save myself…"

"It would be no curse." He leaned closer to whisper in her ear. "Think of the research we could conduct as husband and wife."

Her eyes went wide at his suggestion. When she looked at him he winked. He was much too charming. Her face went hot thinking about what he'd said.

She'd wanted to do those things with him ever since their exploratory kiss, but she didn't dare to think it would ever really happen. But now he was offering to marry her.

"I would not expect such a thing. This is my problem, not yours."

"Marry me, and let it be *our* problem." He seemed so serious, but…

"Are you sure?"

"We must go now before we are found. I can't stop him if he is your guardian instead of me."

"You didn't say you were sure." It was silly, but she needed to hear him say the words. To alleviate just a fraction of her guilt. For she wanted to say yes, and not just because of the threat of her brother taking her to Flint.

"I'm sure, Thea. Are you?"

"Not even a little bit. I fear you will come to resent me some-day for this, but I'm not brave enough to reject your offer."

"I'm glad to know you prefer me to whatever waits in Lon-don."

"Actually… I prefer you by an extremely wide margin," she said, causing him to laugh.

"Then let's hurry before we're caught."

Thea didn't need to be asked again. She held onto Shay's hand as he practically pulled her along behind him toward the front door. She stumbled down the steps, but Shay only leaned down and scooped her up into his arms causing her breath to rush out in a quick gasp.

He settled her on the saddle and in the next breath he hoisted himself up behind her and put the horse toward the village.

They were racing through the field when Thea leaned back slightly, feeling the heat of Shay's body against hers. She was basically sitting on the man's lap. Riding astride pushed her gown up to her thighs where he could easily see the edges of her stockings and her bare skin.

It wouldn't matter once they were married. He'd have the right to any part of her. He'd also have the right to all her earnings.

"I have no dowry, but my earnings will serve as payment," she called loudly enough for him to hear over the wind rushing past their ears.

"Nay. Your money is yours alone, Thea. You've earned every pence through your blood, sweat, and tears and I'll not touch it."

It was more than she could have hoped. She'd never considered marriage because she'd lose control over her funds as well as her time and her body. But Shay was offering her the protection of his name, the pleasure of his body, as well as the security of her future.

"Thank you, Shay."

"I know well how it feels not to have two pennies to rub together. I'd never let ye feel so beholden to another for your well-being."

She felt tears spring to her eyes and it had nothing to do with the stinging wind as he pushed his horse faster. Through her watery sight she saw the first buildings in the village. They were almost there and Stephen was still sitting in the castle.

Shay pulled up right in front of the blacksmith's forge and slid down. Handing the reins off to a small lad who came running, Shay reached up for her and helped her down to her feet.

When she swayed a bit he held tighter until she breathed and nodded.

After flipping a coin to the boy, he took her hand in his. She expected him to pull her toward the anvil sitting out from the flaming embers and smoke. But he paused. Seeing the lump of steel sitting there so innocently, brought the reality of things into sharp focus.

"Shay?" she whispered, the word little more than a breath, but he heard her for he leaned down to look at her. "Are you certain this is what you want? I'm beyond appreciative for your offer, but now that we are here, I must make sure. What if you meet someone you love someday and you are not able to be with her because of me?"

He made a sound that could only be described as a snort and shook his head.

"I've no right to have anyone ever come to love me. Protecting ye, might sway things a bit in my favor if things such as goodness and honor come to be important when a life is over. So ye see? You could be sparing me a bit of heat."

He'd said such things before, but she didn't understand. There was little time now to discuss theology and what happens when we die. But before she could push matters he continued.

"You should know before we do this that there are things in my past that are not pleasant. Things I've done—"

"I know who you are. You are a good man." She glanced toward the anvil and amended her words "You are the very best of men."

"I'm sorry I have no ring and didn't have time to ask ye properly to wed me. But you should know I'm not so sorry to have ye as my bride. I think we will rub along well. It will be a humorous tale to tell our children someday."

"You want this to be a real marriage?" She had not considered these details. Again she glanced at the anvil, feeling the power it held over their lives. Perhaps not the anvil itself as much as the vows they would make while standing over it.

"Aye. I've never planned to marry. I didn't feel it was right. But there is a duty to do so for the man who'd found me starving in Inverness. And I can't think of a better reason to marry than to save another person who needs me. I feel it will redeem a few of my past wrongs." He frowned. "I guess I should have spoken words of love. I'm making a mess of this."

She shook her head and smiled at him. "No. I'd rather have the truth than hollow words, and I'd rather have friendship and safety than a ring."

"I shall give you all of that, Thea. I promise."

She would be a wife and a mother. But he would allow her to write her stories and keep her money. She smiled at this man who'd offered her the life she'd given up on years ago. No. A life she'd never thought to hope for.

THEIR WORDS WERE spoken quickly as they gripped hands over the anvil. When the blacksmith slipped into Gaelic, Shay translated the man's words so Thea could repeat them easily.

In a matter of minutes it was done and Shay had himself a bride. He also had a brother-in-law he needed to run off his lands.

He hoisted her up into the saddle as he'd done earlier and rode for the castle. This time, however, he didn't feel the guilt over enjoying the woman's backside as he urged his horse faster. She was his wife now so anything they did would be sanctioned by the church.

He sighed when he recalled the promise he'd given her. Beyond their vows of loving each other until death, which they both knew was an exaggeration, he'd promised her honesty. But already everything she knew about him was a lie.

He would take care of one problem at a time. First, Stephen would be dealt with, and then he would talk to Thea.

"Can we stop at the cottage?" she asked. He nodded and reined his horse in that direction. He didn't know what she might want to do there before facing her brother, but they had time now. Even if Shay didn't want that rotter in his home for a minute longer than necessary.

He'd hurt Frannie and planned to do the unthinkable with his sister. The man deserved a right thrashing. If he didn't leave them in peace that was what he would get.

Thea's request turned out to be the best thing, for as they stopped in front of the cottage, Shay saw Stephen on the porch, being held from entering by Frannie wielding a fire poker. Billings was pleading with the man to no avail.

"Oh, dear," Thea said as Shay dismounted and helped Thea to her feet. "Frannie," she called. "Please go inside."

Shay might have thought she wished to spare her brother harm, but he knew Thea enough to know it was that she cared for Frannie and didn't want her to have to spend any time in the man's presence.

"He wanted to come in and look for you. But I wouldn't let him, Miss Thea."

"I thank you for your loyalty. You can go in the house. Shay and I will see to him."

"I wanted to—" Frannie began to cry in earnest. "I thought… but I couldn't."

Thea made her way up the steps and took the weapon before wrapping an arm around the shaking girl. "All will be well. Go on inside."

Frannie nodded after another glare in Stephen's direction. When the maid was back inside, Stephen spoke.

"I've been looking everywhere for you, Thea. Damn you for making me come all this way to collect you. But we'll deal with it when we get back to London."

Thea held out the fire poker, resting it on Stephen's chest.

"I don't know what you have learned or how you went about getting the information, but I'm not going anywhere with you. You are no kind of brother to plan to drug me, and give me to Flint to cover your debts. What happened to you, Stephen?"

At least the swine had the grace to look guilty before his reddened face pulled up in anger.

"I am the head of the family and as such, I decide what is to happen with you."

She pressed the point of the poker harder and Stephen yelped before grasping it from her grip and tossing it aside. He reached out to grab her arm.

"You are coming with me. You will do your duty."

"Let go of my wife. You have no authority over her," Shay said firmly.

"Wife?" Stephen swallowed loudly. "No. I didn't give my permission."

"You well know I've reached my majority and can marry if I wish to without your approval. Besides, we're in Scotland which means I could marry even if I weren't of age."

"Damn you, Thea. What have you done? Marrying yourself to him?" Stephen pointed in Shay's direction as if speaking of some foul beast. "People suspect he's not even the actual marquess. There's no way to know for sure, just a dying old man, desperate for an heir to claim him. He's likely nothing more than a gutter rat."

Shay had heard such accusations before, but they never went anywhere. Harrington had made certain everything was sealed and final on his title.

"Your children will be mongrels," Stephen spat.

There'd been a time when Shay had felt guilty for how he'd treated the man, but now…He pushed those thoughts aside.

His brave Valkyrie stepped closer and slapped her brother across the face.

"If you are to be the example of what comes from a superior bloodline, I'm afraid you've fallen far short. I'm surprised the marquess would dare to wed me after knowing what a bounder you are. I care nothing about a person's blood, for it is rarely seen. But I know Shay is more honorable than you, so don't fear for our children except that they have *you* for an uncle."

She was magnificent in her defense of him and the family they didn't have. He could have done with seeing her slap the man again, but Stephen held up a hand.

"Thea, you don't understand," he stressed.

She laughed harshly. "What don't I understand, brother? That you planned to use me in the most hideous of ways all so you might feed your craving to continue gambling? What, pray tell, would you do the next time you owed such a debt? Or the time after that?"

"I know you have money. I don't know where you got it, but you would have paid a fair sum to hire a coach to bring you here. And a fortnight of staying at inns along the way."

"Whatever funds I do or don't have is now the business of my husband. Not you. Please go, Stephen. I don't want to see you ever again. Mama and Papa would be so ashamed of you."

Shay had been standing back, allowing Thea to handle this situation with her brother so she might have some finality of seeing him off once and for all. But even a gutter rat like Shay hadn't expected the man to reach out and grasp his own kin by the neck with the intent of choking the life from her.

Chapter Twenty

T HEA HAD BEEN wrong to think her words might strike some bit of compassion in her brother, but still she hadn't expected him to grab hold of her throat to choke her.

Fortunately, Shay was close enough to come to her rescue, yet again. After pulling Stephen's hand away from her, he punched her brother in the face, laying him right out on the ground.

Shay pointed to the lump on the ground. "Billings, please take your friend away from here before I cause him more damage."

Lord Billings frowned and stepped up to Thea.

"You should know, my lady, I had tried to talk him out of this plan. I only came with him in the hope I might save you such a fate."

"I thank you. Unfortunately, the viscount has become too desperate in his sickness to do what is right," Thea explained something she was certain Billings knew well already.

"I would strongly encourage you to sever all ties with him once you're back in London," Shay added. "His future is uncertain."

Thea felt a twinge of sickness in her stomach at Shay's words. She was not an innocent ninny, she understood well enough what could happen to her brother when all hope of paying his debts had passed, but the finality of it…

This was her brother. She shook her head as she rubbed at the soreness along her throat. Proof he was no longer any kind of brother. She'd known for some time the sweet, funny, boy she remembered had left her.

"Yes. That is good advice," Billings answered as he attempted to get the other man up.

His butler and housekeeper came running.

"M'lord, he wouldn't stay at the castle. He insisted on coming to the cottage." Mrs. Murray tilted her head at Stephen. "It seems you took care of him, ye did."

"Aye. John, will you fetch our guest's conveyance and have it brought down so the viscount can be loaded up and taken back to London? Mrs. Murray, Frannie is inside the house. Would you please see to her and make sure she's well?"

"Aye. Right away," the Murrays said at the same time as they hurried off in different directions. But not before Mrs. Murray stopped to squeeze her arm.

"All will be well now, lass."

But would that be true? She was now married to a man who'd never wanted a wife. He seemed pleased now, but what might happen later when he'd had time to think on it?

At that moment he had come up behind her, supporting her as if he worried she might faint.

She smiled up at him. "Thank you, but I'm not one for swooning," she assured him.

"I wouldn't have expected it. You're far stronger than him." Shay cast a sneer in the direction of her brother who had let out a moan as he began to come round. "Still, I'll see you safely inside."

Instead of going to the drawing room he took her into the dining room she'd never used. He helped her into one of the elaborate chairs and went to the sideboard where he poured her a glass of whisky larger than she'd seen civilized people drink. She didn't argue when he placed it in her shaking hands.

"It is over now. You are safe. No one will ever hurt you, I

promise."

"It is strange how I'm able to manage an ordeal as it happens only to fall apart when it's over." She chuckled but the sound seemed forced.

"I would say that's better than the other way around." He winked and placed a soft kiss on her temple before he turned for the door. "I'll be back after seeing to..." He waved toward the front of the house and Thea knew what he meant.

She took a sip of the strong liquid and coughed before taking another one. While the burn in her throat was uncomfortable, the warmth in her belly soothed her frayed nerves.

She'd never expected her life to take on the plot of one of her books. So many days she'd sat in her room at Percival House writing of adventure while her life was as unexciting as a white handkerchief. It seemed the only thing missing now was a hungry crocodile.

STEPHEN RALLIED SLIGHTLY when he was dumped into the carriage with little decorum from Shay. Shay couldn't bring himself to be gentle with a man who would treat his sister so abdominally. The man was a disgrace. Thea had been right, that having a pure bloodline didn't ensure the person was honorable.

He smiled thinking how much of his life would now be taken up by Thea being right. Shay had seen the way Finn conceded to Lily when she said something more astute. There was no resentment when Finn was proved wrong on something.

How surprised they would be to learn Shay had married. He knew they would be as happy as he was. And Shay was happy about the situation. It was new and he'd probably never have considered it if Stephen hadn't forced his hand. For that, Shay should be grateful to the rotter, but he wouldn't be thanking him anytime soon.

"Will you...?" Stephen's breath caught on a pathetic sob before he tried again. "Will you take care of her, Flemming? Please? Make sure she's safe."

Shay looked over his shoulder toward the house where his new wife was sitting inside with a stout glass of whisky he'd given her. He was fortunate she had not wanted to join him to see her brother off, for this display would surely be confusing for such an adoring sister. To hear Stephen worry over Thea showed a small glimpse of the man he'd once had been. Before the vicious vines of his addiction had pulled him under.

"I will see her happy," Shay said when what he'd wanted to do was lash out by saying, "She'll surely be happier with me than with the life you'd planned for her." But there was nothing to come from such accusations.

Shay had seen this sickness with men who couldn't pass up the table or a drink or even a woman. There was no denying how badly Stephen wanted to be that brother. But he didn't have the strength to fight off the demons haunting his life now. Few did.

Shay watched the carriage until it couldn't be seen and then turned for the house. It wasn't until his foot came down on the first step that he felt the weight of what had transpired today.

He'd married Thea.

She'd said she was selfish for accepting his offer, but now as the repercussions settled in, he realized he was the selfish one. He'd married her under false pretenses. He'd lied to her as he'd lied to everyone else. She didn't even know him.

Perhaps it wasn't such a strange thing to be strong in the height of a crisis but crumble once the dust had settled. He'd done what he needed to do to protect Thea, but now he would need to find a way to tell her the truth.

To share a part of him he'd never told another soul.

WHEN STEPHEN WAS gone, Thea felt as if she'd been awake for three weeks straight, but it was not quite time for supper. How could that be?

She wandered back to the drawing room and took her seat at her desk. She'd been writing the scene where the hero prevailed when Shay had come rushing in with the news and it felt like someone else had written it.

In just a few hours' time she'd married a man she'd fantasized about for weeks. She looked at that man now as he came into the drawing room. Her husband.

"Let us sit, there is much to discuss," Shay suggested. He gestured toward the settee where he'd spent many hours reading and dozing off.

As exhausted as she was, she knew she wouldn't be at risk of falling asleep during this conversation.

He took the seat next to her, so close their legs touched. She looked up at his face, drawn in seriousness. Was he already regretting their marriage?

As he'd said, there was much to discuss. So much, in fact, she didn't know where to start, so she just sat there looking at her hands twisting the fabric of her gown.

When he didn't say anything either, she imagined he, too, was at a loss. She risked a glance at him at the same time he looked at her and when he smiled, she couldn't help but grin back. Then something else seemed to take over and a chuckle broke free. Shay laughed and soon they were both laughing uncontrollably. She wiped at the tears streaking down her face.

After such an emotional day she wasn't surprised to be dealing with tears, but them being from laughter was quite a shock.

Eventually their mirth died down to a few deep breaths and the marquess spoke.

"I have a wife. That is not something I ever expected to say. Yet, I find I'm not displeased about it. I like you a great deal. And truth be told, I've wanted you in my bed for some time. Even before the kiss, I'd dreamed of you."

He was so confident. He seemed at ease to just say what he felt. She decided she wanted to be like that as well. And what danger was there in agreeing with the man.

"I feel the same way. In fact, I even wrote a story about the things I thought of doing with you."

Shay winced and she wanted to assure him, but didn't know what he'd found fault in.

"I know of the story. I read it." His wince wasn't from disgust, but guilt.

"But... how?"

"It was in a stack of pages. At first I just thought it was out of order, but then I realized it wasn't part of the golden feather story at all. Perhaps it would have been honorable if I'd stopped reading once I learned it wasn't for my eyes, but I'm sorry, knowing only made me want to study every swirl of every letter. It was lovely, if ... incomplete."

Incomplete.

They kissed.

Except at the time she'd not been able to write about the kiss for she'd never experienced such a thing. Now she had. And she hoped now that she was his wife she might have other experiences. Things that would never be written on a page for being too erotic. She knew there were such books, but Theodore Stonecliff wouldn't write one.

Shay was staring at her lips again and her body leaned closer without her having to consciously think to do so. But her movement seemed to startle him out of his trance.

"You should move to the castle."

"Oh." She looked around the room of her borrowed home. She'd hoped to have found a place similar, but now she did not need to buy a home for herself. Her home would be with Lord Flemming.

"Not to worry, the marchioness's rooms boast a large study that looks out over the garden. As I recall the desk is rather small, but we can have this one moved up, or better yet, I will commission a new one that is big enough for your needs."

She blinked, shocked into silence by his kindness. Not only had he saved her from a life of danger and unhappiness, but he knew her secret and was willing to modify his home so she might continue writing. It was more than she could have hoped for. A husband who would understand, and accept her. But Shay more than accepted her, he encouraged her.

Tears came again, not from laughter this time but with relief.

"Lord Flemming, I cannot—"

"Shay," he interrupted her with is given name.

"Shay." She nodded. "I cannot thank you enough for what you have done today. I thought only of evading my brother, but now that the events of the day have settled in I realize it is more than that. You have given me your name, your protection, a home." She took a breath. "Safety."

"It was not without some selfishness, Thea. Please don't make me out to be the hero in one of your books. I don't want this to be a marriage in name only. I also desperately want you in my bed. And maybe I offered for you out of desperation to keep you safe, but I do hope you will allow me to assist in your research of more… carnal topics."

Her face flushed hot. If this had been a traditional marriage with plans and preparations she would have had time to arrange her wedding night. But this morning when she'd woke, marriage was the furthest thing from her mind. And now she was a bride.

She nodded and smiled so he might know she wanted the same thing, without needing the courage to speak on it.

"Frannie," he called. The maid came rushing in.

"Aye, my lord?" The girl was back to not looking at him. In fact, she didn't look at Thea either, keeping her gaze upon the floor in front of them.

"Are you well from your scare today?" he asked quietly.

"Aye, my lord. I am so sorry I couldn't…"

"It is over. You are safe. So is Thea. That's all that matters. Well that, and knowing if you would be up to making us a tray of food so we can retire upstairs."

"Straight away, my lord. I'd be happy to."

"Thank you, Frannie," Shay said, though he doubted Frannie had heard as quickly as she'd hurried from the room to see to her task.

Shay turned his attention back to Thea and she got caught in his blue gaze.

"I thought you may want to stay one last night in your room here."

She laughed. "You did not want to have to wait for us to make our way up to the castle," she guessed at the real reason he was content to stay here with only the one servant and a tray of meat and cheese instead of a full meal.

"My but you know me so well already, wife." He paused. "Did that sound as strange as it did for me to say it?"

"I'm sure it did."

"We will have time to get used to it."

"Yes," she agreed. They would have the rest of their lives to get used to it or spend the rest of their days in regret.

Chapter Twenty-One

SHAY FELT AS if he had been picked up in a storm funnel and set back down in the same place while everything else in his life had gone completely sideways. He was a husband. Something he'd never thought to be.

Something he shouldn't have been so selfish as to have done. Thea was happy now. Thanking him even. But if she knew the truth... If she knew who he was, she would likely not be so happy.

It was easy enough for him to use her worm of a brother as an excuse. Marrying Thea had ended that threat once and for all. But Shay was not so deluded about his honor to know he had other reasons. And the reason at the top of his list was about to happen forthwith.

He took his wife's hand and led her up the stairs. It had been so long since he'd been upstairs in the cottage, it took him a moment to remember which was the dowager's chamber and which were for guests.

Thea helpfully pointed in the right direction.

The room was tidy and he wondered if she was ever in it long enough to disturb anything but the bedcovers. And even those were not touched every night, for he knew on occasion she fell asleep at her writing desk. And other times she got up early when she couldn't sleep.

He knew a lot of intimate details about Theodora Sutton Buchanan, Marchioness Flemming, but what he desperately wanted to know tonight was what she looked like when she took her pleasure.

He wanted to see the color of the blush on her cheeks and hear her moans of desire. What he wished he didn't have to hear was his name. Or rather the name he'd gone by since he was eleven years of age. Not now when they were about to consummate a marriage neither expected, but perhaps both of them secretly wanted.

He couldn't think of any way around it. He'd given her leave of using it, rather than have her shouting "Lord Flemming" as she reached climax. That would have been awkward and unsettling indeed. Still, for this moment he wished for anything she would whisper his real name.

The name his mother had given him when he was born. But, alas, that was impossible for many reasons.

He stroked the side of her face with the back of his hand.

"Ye are lovely," he said because it was true and because a bride on her wedding night should hear such words.

"So are you." She closed her eyes. "Handsome, I mean." She laughed. "For all my command of the written word, I still have difficulty wrangling the correct words when I speak."

"Neither of us need speak very much if we are kissing."

She nodded quickly as if she'd been eagerly waiting.

He leaned down to press his lips to hers. Like the day they'd been doing their research, he allowed himself to get caught up for there were no lessons to be taught or points to be made. Just them coming together in the most divine way.

He reached for his cravat and was about to pull it away when a timid knock on the door interrupted them.

Thea blinked at him as if unaware of who it might be. Shay went to the door and opened it wide enough to take the tray and thank Frannie for the food.

"That will be all," Shay said to make sure the girl knew they wished to be alone for the rest of the evening.

Thea looked at the tray as it was set it on a table and then to him. He wondered if she was hungry and wished to eat first, but she stepped closer to him and initiated their kiss. Leaning up on tip-toes to put her hand on his cheek and pull him to her.

He went willingly and gave all the power over to her to explore and lead them along the connection. Her tongue reached out to touch his and he responded, curling his into her mouth.

She moaned in such a way his cock throbbed against his trews. He restrained himself a little longer before allowing his hands to float over her back and then around to her breasts.

She gasped and pulled away to look at him.

"No?" he asked when she didn't say anything. Did she not want to be touched there?

"Yes," she answered. "Yes," she repeated when he didn't move to touch her again.

"You may touch me wherever you wish as well," he encouraged and she didn't waste any time reaching up to run both hands up over his chest to his shoulders.

She made quick work of the loosened knot of his cravat and pulling it off. He'd done away with his coat downstairs but she unbuttoned his waistcoat and slid it off of him as well.

He turned her so he could make haste with her buttons. Her gown slid down her body and he looked at the threadbare shift she wore underneath. It was naught but a bunch of strings clinging to one another. While he hated that she had not been afforded the things she should have, he was at least grateful for the view this garment was unable to hide from him.

"You shall have new shifts on the morrow. Pretty silk," he promised her. For a moment he wondered why she had not bought them herself. Some indulgence her brother would never see. But he knew she would not have enjoyed such a thing before. Luxurious shifts wouldn't have made up for the anxiety over losing one's home at any moment.

She would never need to worry over such a thing ever again. She was free.

And he wanted to extend that freedom to what happened between them in bed.

He removed his boots, stockings, and trews next as she watched. The flare of interest and desire in her eyes communicated how much she liked what she saw and it made him ache even more. When he reached behind his head to pull his shirt over his head, she gasped.

She looked away with a maiden's blush on her cheeks, but not before he'd seen the shock.

"It is proportionate then?" she said. "To your size."

He pressed his lips together so not to laugh. She was always researching even if he knew this particular topic would never make it onto the pages of one of her books. She was curious and he enjoyed being able to answer her questions.

"I can't say that I've seen many besides my own. So I don't know for sure. But it would stand that since I'm larger than most men everywhere else I'd be larger there as well."

"Well, I've only seen one."

When he cocked his head she explained.

"Lord Billings. After a night of drink with my brother he seemed to have lost possession of his clothes and his mind for he was walking about the house in nothing but his stockings. It was nothing like this."

"As rewarding as this discussion is for my ego, I find I'm not so insecure to need it to continue. I'd rather you only thought of one man's cock this evening."

She laughed and nodded.

"Please forgive me. I will trust that you know best. After all you've done this many times in the past and I'm to assume you never permanently injured anyone or you would have boasted about it by now."

He hung his head and shook it with a chuckle. "We are getting completely off course. You're not to be thinking about the other women or Billings's cock. We should only be thinking about us. Here. Now."

"You're right. I'm just nervous. I'm sorry."

"Nothing to be sorry for. I'll take care of you, Thea. In all things."

She nodded. "It's so strange to not be alone."

He kissed her again, getting them back on track. When she touched him, she followed the same trail she'd used before. This time, however, her cool fingers trailed over his bare skin leaving goosebumps in their path.

He deepened the kiss and untied the thin, frayed ribbon at her bosom before he realized there was no reason to be gentle with this garment since its replacement was nigh. He recalled her writing about the hero ripping the woman's shift.

Pulling away slightly, he grinned before grasping the fabric with both hands and rending it down the front. She gasped but her eyes darkened with lust at his show of ferocity. He may need to get her an entire coach of shifts for this garment would probably not be the last casualty.

He kissed her hard and she kept up, her touch drifted down his back, lower until her palms fit against his arse. Then with more confidence than any other virgin might have had, she slid her hand around his hip to his front and grasped him.

Despite him scolding Thea for thinking about other people, Shay was unable to stop himself from comparing her touch to all the others before her. If only to wonder why it was so different when his new bride touched him. He was no green lad, he'd had pleasure in a myriad of ways but this simple touch nearly unmanned him.

He held her slim wrist to make the agony stop.

"Did I do something wrong?" she asked.

"Nay. Not at all. It is lovely that you wish to touch me. It feels good. Too good and I want to last for you." As well as for him.

"I don't know what you mean."

Right. She wouldn't understand that part. He opened his

mouth ready to explain like he did with all her questions but then he smiled and took her hand in his.

"Let me show you," he said instead before leading her to the bed.

Chapter Twenty-Two

THEA'S THOUGHTS WERE a blur. It felt as if she'd had too much whisky, something she'd done only once, for research. Everything seemed hazy, and dreamlike. The light from the candles was soft and made the room warm. Or maybe that was her husband's body. Everywhere she'd touched him he felt like a flame. Especially the silken member between his legs.

She'd not expected it to feel that way. Not that she'd thought much on how it should have felt. All of this was so new. She didn't want to miss any detail.

Shay lay out in the bed after pulling the coverings off. He patted the mattress next to him and offered an inviting smile before holding out his hand toward her.

Her delay in joining him was not because she had any doubts, for there was no room in her head for such things. She only paused so to take in his beauty. He might not have liked that word used to describe his body, but it was the only word she could come up with. She'd known he was large, of course, anyone could see the way his coats strained across his wide shoulders despite being fitted for him particularly. And the way his thighs stretched the fabric of his breeches especially when he was sitting a horse.

But she'd not realized under his clothes were rolling hills and valleys of muscle. Especially across his stomach, and lower, where that large part of him seemed to lurch out at her from the black hair that seemed confined to that part of his body just like hers, but so very different.

His legs seemed to go on forever, and like those afternoons when he'd stretched out on her settee to nap, his feet hung over the edge. No doubt his bed in the castle would have been made for someone of his size. Plus another person.

He shifted across the space she was to take up and reached for her again. This time she went.

The linens were already warm from his body, not that she spent much time feeling them. Shay wrapped his arm around her and rolled her over on top of him.

She'd only seen the way men and women came together in a drawing she'd come across in the margin of a book. But it depicted the woman being on the bottom while the man lay between her legs.

This position was, however, more suitable for kissing. For she didn't need to reach up to touch his lips. In fact, she needed to bend her head down the slightest bit. He slid her legs to the sides of his body so her thighs rested by his hips and she felt that hard bulge at the very place it was somehow supposed to enter her body.

But it was his fingers that reached between them stroking her as she had done to herself on occasion, but oh so much better. His touch found the very place she wanted him and he focused there. Stroking and pressing in the most delightful way as she panted to catch her breath. And then those talented fingers slipped inside her, filling her exquisitely. Even as he kept his rhythm in that other place.

The two sensations together were too much and she felt her body tightening and she knew what would happen but had never felt it so intensely before.

When her climax came, she couldn't help but cry out in pleasure. While she was still shaking he lifted her slightly and placed the tip of him at the opening that still throbbed.

"This is for you to take when you are ready," he said.

She shook her head, not understanding. Not only was her mind rather useless at the moment but she recalled the drawing and knew this wasn't how it worked.

He nodded as if she'd said some bit of that out loud.

"You have had little say over your life for the last several years, and in this I want you to have complete control. You will decide when you want to take this next step—and Lord, I pray it is soon before I expire—it is for you."

She wanted him inside her then. Needed him there.

"I'm just to move down?" she asked to be sure this was right.

"Yes. It may hurt, but it should be easier now."

Again she didn't know what he meant, but she trusted him to know. Not just because he had far more experience than her in such things, but that she knew he would want her to feel good.

And he was giving her this power to make it good for her. While it was clear he was in some pain for having to wait for her slow pace.

She edged down slightly and his breath caught as his eyes pinched shut. Yes, definitely some kind of torture for him. She didn't want him to ache like she had. She wanted to give him the same joy he'd given her.

Allowing her body to relax, she slid further down until she felt the discomfort he'd mentioned. It was not so awful, the slickness of her body eased her way until she settled all the way down.

Shay was gasping, but he smiled up at her.

"All right?" he asked.

She waited a brief moment so it would be true when she nodded and said, "Yes."

"When you are ready, you can move."

She did, moving her hips she slid up and then back down slowly at first but then faster as her body decided the pace for itself. Each time she slid down the tension built higher and higher.

"Oh, Shay. Please?" she asked, though she didn't know what she was asking for exactly. It didn't matter he must have understood.

Shay's hands on her hips gripped her tighter until she began to throb once again. He pushed up from the bed to fill her completely as he burst inside of her.

Collapsing on his chest, she felt his heart racing like hers.

"That was magnificent," she said, still floating in that dream-like state that had transformed to a peace that was now drawing her to sleep.

"It was," Shay agreed. His voice rumbled under her ear when he spoke, but she couldn't comment for she was being pulled under. Her exhaustion from such an eventful day caught up with her and she gave in.

SHAY REACHED FOR the coverings and with his foot to assist, managed to get them up over the two of them. She'd fallen asleep on him, so tired she must have been from everything that had transpired. Still he enjoyed the soft weight of her body on his, and the heat still surrounding him for he'd yet to pull free from her.

Such an odd thing that he did not want to. He'd much prefer to stay connected to her while they slept, but soon enough his body betrayed him and he slipped free. He managed to shift them into a more comfortable position but Thea nestled closer into his side as if she'd always slept there and knew her place.

He felt his own body pulling him to join her, but there were so many other things on his mind. The one thing that wouldn't seem to leave him alone was the memory of the way she'd called out his name when she climaxed. It should have been a joyful moment, and it had been. But it was bittersweet for the fact that she had used his name. Or rather the name he'd claimed as his.

He'd hoped his wife would have cried out to some nonspecific deity rather than use a name that was a lie between them.

He thought of the secrets she kept and had shared with him, and knew at some point he would need to tell Thea the truth about him. But not tonight.

He rested for a few hours but woke when Thea moved in her sleep. He wasn't used to sleeping with someone else. His other encounters had been limited to sex and then he'd gone on his way after a bit of tenderness afterward. But he'd not spent the night with anyone. Afraid his dreams would betray him and someone would know his truth.

Thea had shifted to the other side in her sleep and he pressed his body against the bare skin of her back. His growing erection slipped unerringly between her thighs, rousing him to full hardness.

He placed soft kisses on her shoulder and neck, the edge of her ear and she murmured as her movements turned more intentional.

"Shay," she whispered, needy.

That was the permission he needed to redirect himself into her body. Her groan echoed his own as he began moving slow and deep. His hand traced up the side of her body to hold her breast, using his finger to tease the tight peak.

Soon she was thrusting back to meet his every moment forward.

"Thea," he said urgently when his vision began to fracture and his spine heated with his need to let go.

An incoherent moan was her only reply as her body spasmed tightly around his. He drove into her twice more before giving over to his desire.

"So many ways," she muttered. Or at least that's what he thought she'd said.

"Pardon?" he asked but she didn't answer. She was already asleep again.

When morning intruded upon them Thea raised her head to prop it on his chest seeming in no hurry to get out of bed to ready themselves for the day. He was content to stay in bed loving her for as long as his body complied, but they would need food soon enough if they meant to exert so much energy.

The tray Frannie had brought them had been devoured in the wee hours of the morning after she'd woken him to make love to her yet again. But there was nothing left now but crumbs and he knew the ewer was empty of water for he'd used it to clean her delicate skin.

With a sigh he smiled at her. "I'm afraid we will have to get up and see to things today before we starve."

"In the stories, the man goes out to hunt to provide sustenance for his mate."

"What stories are those?" he asked, knowing he would gladly go forage for food for his mate. Especially since he need only dress and go call for Frannie to bring it up.

"Well, not stories, per se, but one story that I read. For research. It was about chimpanzees."

"Are you likening me to a monkey, dear wife?"

Rather than answer, she broke into a fit of giggles that warmed his heart. He may not have wanted this or thought he deserved it, but he was going to find a way to enjoy it.

He pulled on his clothes from yesterday and kissed Thea.

"I am going to the castle to ready for the day. I'll return with the carriage to gather you and your things shortly."

She bit her bottom lip in that way she did when she worried over something.

"What is it?"

"I am to be your marchioness," she said in wonder.

"Aye, but don't worry over it, there's not much to it. You must only see to my every pleasure and never argue with anything I say."

She laughed again. "I believe I have failed already."

"Hmm, I imagine it is too late to do anything about it now. You are well and truly mine, so we'll find a way to carry on."

With another kiss that nearly led to them getting caught up in bed yet again, he bid her goodbye for the moment.

"I'll return within the hour." That should be enough time for her to pack up her things as she didn't have much.

He walked slowly up to the castle, taking note of every bloom and puffy cloud in the sky. Everything seemed brighter and happier this morning. How many times had he walked by these things and not even noticed as he was in a hurry to get to her drawing room. And now she was his.

He'd been jesting when he said she was responsible for his every pleasure, but a great deal of their future happiness or misery would come from being with one another. He planned to do all in his power to make her new life as his marchioness a joyful one.

Which made him think again of the secrets he was keeping from her. Who he was and what he did when he was in London put everything between them at risk. He'd resolved himself to telling her his true identity, but the other piece… he didn't know if she'd be as accepting.

Which meant he needed to sell *Nuit Noire* straight away so she'd never find out.

◆

Chapter Twenty-Three

FRANNIE PACKED THEA'S gowns and things while Thea gathered up her pages as well as her ink, quills, and paper. The maid had been quiet and Thea wasn't sure if she was still uneasy after seeing Stephen yesterday, or if she'd been scandalized by whatever sounds they'd made the night before in her room.

While Frannie's rooms were downstairs, it was still not a large home.

There was nothing for it, and since Thea was at that moment thinking of her husband and wondering when she might get him alone to make those loud noises again, it seemed Thea held no remorse whatsoever.

She went back to seeing to the stacks of papers, making sure they were in order and bound tightly so there was no danger of losing so much as a word. She'd yet to speak to Shay about how much time she would be allowed to work. He'd been most understanding, even asking Mrs. Murray to keep on with her running of the household so Thea could see to her own endeavors. It was so freeing to have someone who knew what she was doing and was pleased to help her continue. She had not realized when she'd been traveling north how much her life would change.

She hoped only for freedom and safety, but now she'd found…

Well, she wasn't exactly sure what word would be best used to describe what was between Shay and herself. Friendship surely. But she thought there was more to it. She'd have time later to deliberate. At times when she was writing and a word evaded her, she put the closest word to the one she was thinking about in its place and came back later to change it when she'd figured it out.

She would do the same in this instance. And friendship was a fine placeholder until she teased out the correct term.

She placed a full bottle of ink inside the box and carried her most prized possessions outside.

Shay took some of her burden when she stepped out of the cottage toward the carriage. He smiled and she couldn't help but grin in return. Even the hour she'd been away from him had seemed too long. How had she become such a silly romantic from speaking a few hasty words over an anvil?

It didn't matter how or why, but it had happened. And now she was moving to live in a castle. Just like the stories her mother told her when she was a little girl. How happy her parents would have been to see Thea so happy.

It seemed strange to have a carriage to take them to the castle she could see on the hill, but it was likely a longer distance than it looked, and would have been made more so for having to carry everything.

Still it took almost as long to load it as it did to traverse the distance.

When they arrived at the castle the servants were all standing in a line along the stone steps awaiting the arrival of their new mistress. Thea had to think back to her training years ago and summon the information she would need to run a home of this size. How would she have time to finish her book if she had to see to meal selections, and household ledgers.

"This is Mrs. Murray the housekeeper."

"Yes. We've met," Thea said when Shay introduced her to

the formidable woman. She'd been kind yesterday when she'd gone to see to Frannie.

"Mayhap we can set aside some time to go over things?" Anna Murray requested, looking neither pleased or displeased about such a thing.

"Yes. That would be most appreciated."

"Mrs. Murray, my wife has other obligations that will keep her from taking over the household, and unless she disagrees, I believe we would both want you to remain in charge of everything." Shay looked at Thea and she smiled and nodded. It was kind of him to think of such a thing.

"If you would not mind, Mrs. Murray."

Mrs. Murray beamed proudly. "It is no bother at all. I've been taking care of this house since I was only two and twenty. I wouldn't know what to do with myself."

Thea relaxed. "Thank you. I would still like to sit with you and get to know you better, if you have the time."

Mrs. Murray nodded. "Aye. I'll arrange it."

When they were inside, Thea paused in awe of the high ceilings of the foyer. She'd known it would be impressive. It was a castle after all and a castle by definition was the most elaborate of dwellings. She'd expected it to be beautiful, but she also saw the strength of the stone arches. The warmth in the tapestries that hung on the walls showing depictions of sea journeys and starry nights.

"If there is anything you wish to change in the house, you should do so. I want this to be your home," Shay said.

She shook her head. "It is beautiful."

He waved a hand. "I know which room you wish to see first. Come." He held out his hand and she took it so he could lead her up the curved stairs to the second floor. Down the heavily carpeted corridor he stopped at the end. The double doors on the left were heavy looking with carved, dark wood. Thea almost expected to see iron braces ready to hold a bar across them. The double doors on the other side were softer in some way. Still with designs carved into wood, but lighter.

"The marchioness's rooms." He opened the door into a small sitting room. Then through another set of doors into a study. He'd been right when he said the desk was small.

Before she could tell him she would make it work, he had rung for a footman.

"Cragen, I'd like the settee from my study brought up and changed out with this one. And for now, bring up the desk from library. The one that sits to the left of the door when you enter. I believe it will be more suited for the marchioness's needs."

Every time she heard him refer to her as the marchioness, she felt a little thrill of excitement that faded with a bit of unease. She was a marchioness now. No longer a spinster. Oh, how happy she was to never hear that term again.

Shay took the items from her arms and began setting them on the smaller desk he'd moved to the wall to make room by the window.

"I know you like to have a window to look out of as you write." He turned toward the door as the first piece of furniture was brought in. A large settee.

"Put it here, and take this smaller piece away." To her he said. "This one was much too dainty for me to nap on."

It was true, the legs were even more fragile looking than the settee in her old drawing room.

"Through that door is the bed chamber, but you shan't need that," he said surely.

She wasn't sure if he meant for her to sleep with him as she had the night before, or if he meant she spent many nights asleep at her desk. Thea didn't ask.

Later that afternoon, when all her things were now put away in the castle, Thea met with Mrs. Murray in the solar. Thea found the housekeeper, Anna, to be a delightful woman who had many stories of the marquess when he'd first come to Cawdor.

"He was such a small lad. I feel directly responsible for the size he is now, for I couldn't look into those big blue eyes and not succumb to giving him more sweets. Back when he first came here, Master Buchanan could not seem to get enough to eat. And when there was any bit of chill in the air you would find him cozied up to a fire in some room of the house. He doesn't like to be cold, that one."

Thea's heart broke for the boy he'd been. Even knowing how hale and hearty he was now, she could imagine him frail and starving. A child alone in the cold world.

"I don't know how he survived so long on his own. I was seven and ten when my parents left me and I didn't know much about taking care of myself. How he did it as a mere child, I don't know."

"He's a survivor. Though he is not without his scars."

Thea looked at the woman, not understanding. She'd studied near to every inch of Shay's body the night before and hadn't seen much in the way of scars. No more than anyone else had, she guessed.

"He was prone to night terrors as a boy," Mrs. Murray went on to explain. "Calling out for his mother or others for help. The staff would find him sleeping in different rooms, usually in the corners, shivering and whimpering. It broke my heart. My dear husband has carried the marquess to his bed on many occasions. Though more recently, he's not able to be carried." Mrs. Murray smiled. "I'm to understand the gang of boys Shay ran with in Inverness became his family. While they hadn't always stayed on the right side of the law, they found a way to keep food in their bellies and I'll not judge them for what they'd had to do. Any one of us would have done the same when faced with such dire circumstances."

Thea nodded, understanding more than what Mrs. Murray might have thought. Thea had turned to writing under a man's name to support herself and her brother as best she could. If she'd been found out she would have been ruined, though she didn't know how much lower her family's name could fall.

"I don't blame him either," Thea said because it was clear

Mrs. Murray needed to hear Thea say as much. "Everything he went through is the reason he is the man he is today, so while we can wish he'd had an easier beginning, I wouldn't want him any other way."

Mrs. Murray smiled and patted Thea's hand. "You are good for him. I know you didn't wed under the best of terms but I think it's the only way he would have ever done it. Even before you married I could see a change in him when he went down to the cottage to visit you. I think you did not have such an easy life living with that brother of yours in London, and while I'd not wish such a thing on anyone, I'm glad that it made you come here."

After a moment of silence, Mrs. Murray added, "I think it would make a good story, and I hear from Frannie you are writing a story." She put her hands up. "I don't need any details, mind ye. It may be an unconventional thing for a lady to do, but the marquess does love a good tale so it seems a perfect match to me."

"Thank you, Mrs. Murray for accepting me. And for keeping on with the castle so I can manage my other responsibilities. If there is anything you need from me, please let me know. I don't like to think I am not doing my duty."

"Many like to think they know what another's duty ought to be, but I think they'd be better to keeping their noses in their own business and let us do what is right for our home, aye?"

"Aye," Thea agreed with a smile, using the foreign word.

Mrs. Murray laughed. "Very good. We'll make a proper Scottish lass of ye yet, Lady Flemming."

Over the next few days, Thea settled into her new life at the castle. Writing most of the day.

Shay came in and took his place on the larger settee in the late mornings. And then they shared the noon meal together before he would go into his own study to take care of business.

But in the evenings she retired to her own bedchamber alone.

She'd wanted to be invited into his room so they might spend their nights much like they had their first as a married couple, but he never extended the request for her company. And she hadn't been brave enough to ask him.

Perhaps that was how married life was supposed to be. She didn't remember if her parents had spent their nights in the same chamber or not. Not that she would compare. This marriage was between Shay and her and wasn't for anyone else to say what was right or not.

Now that she'd talked to Mrs. Murray though, Thea wondered if maybe the reason he'd not asked her to stay with him had been because of his restless dreams.

She would have to find a way to broach the topic though, for her body, despite never being touched previously, had become needy for her husband's attention.

She sat at her desk and took up her quill waiting for Lord Flemming to arrive so she might pounce. The man had gone to great measures to not be trapped, but he was about to walk right into hers.

Chapter Twenty-Four

As he'd done before Thea had moved up to the castle and taken over the marchioness's rooms, Shay stood at the doorway watching her as she wrote. Unlike when she'd lived in the cottage, his arrival was not announced by his heavy boots on the wooden porch. Instead, thick carpet in the hallway muted his steps and he was able to watch her longer than he'd been able to before.

She was beautiful, despite the shabby gown and messy hair. He knew under the gown would be a new shift, silky and adorned with the best French lace. He was certain because he'd purchased them for her himself and instructed Frannie to get rid of her other tattered garments. New gowns would arrive soon enough but it was those shifts that intrigued him.

He'd not gotten the chance to see them yet, though they'd been prominent in his recent fantasies.

For a moment he thought Thea had escaped a smudge of ink that morning, but then he saw it, on her wrist today. Seeing it brought a smile to his face, just as his wife looked up to catch him there.

"Good morning, my lord."

He made a noise and waved his hand. "No need to be so formal. I plan to call you by your name. Thea."

He enjoyed seeing the shiver shake her shoulders.

"And what would you like me to call you? Dearest husband?"

"It is rather long. Might I suggest, *the god who makes my legs tremble with desire?*"

"Yes. That is quite a bit shorter. I should have thought of it." She laughed.

He stepped closer and cleared his throat.

"I have something for you."

"Oh? A present? Was the castle not enough?"

He shook his head feeling nervous, and held out the ring. There was no box and he realized then he could have gotten one before now, but it was too late now.

Thea gasped as she looked down at the ring, a pearl locked inside a knot.

"It's beautiful."

"You will have access to the Flemming jewels as is your station, but this piece belonged to my mother." What he couldn't say was that it had never been part of the Flemming jewels.

"Thank you. I will cherish it always." She smiled as she slipped it on her finger. But his nerves kicked up again when the smile faded slightly.

"What is it?" he asked. If she didn't like it he would get her whatever she wanted. Anything to make her happy.

"You've not invited me to your bed since we married. Did I do something wrong? If so, you need only guide me in how you would prefer—"

"Thea," he interrupted because he couldn't stand to let another second go by with her thinking she had displeased him in some way. Not when quite the opposite was true. Leave it to his new wife to just blurt out the thing that had been silent this last week. What she lacked in size, she made up for in courage. It was time for him to be as brave. "You have pleased me in all ways. That is not…"

He paused, realizing he'd inadvertently traversed into an area he hadn't planned to discuss. Not yet.

"I must admit," she said, "I have thought of little else. I don't know how I'll manage to finish this book when I don't give a damn about who has the blasted feather."

He laughed at her language. It was not the first time he'd heard her curse, but for some reason he enjoyed hearing such coarse words on her tongue. His body stirred and he wondered if she'd done that on purpose.

Perhaps women were born with inherent instincts on how to lure a man to his doom. Like a flower's sweetness lured the honeybee. Her honesty was yet another thing that brought him closer to her desk.

"I want you just as much," he admitted for he was not going to be weak when his wife was so brave.

"Then you have no regrets on marrying me yet?" she asked. She smiled, but he could tell this had been on her mind. Damn his inattention for making her think such a thing.

"There's nothing I regret except not making sure you knew how wonderful you are."

"But you've not asked me to your rooms." Thea was not one to back away until she'd gotten to the heart of the matter. He would tell her the parts he was comfortable with, at least.

"You've been writing long into the night and I didn't want to disrupt."

She tilted her head to the side in a challenging expression before standing.

"You have disrupted me nearly every day of our acquaintance until we married, why would the evenings be different?" She stepped around the desk and he couldn't help but look toward the door so to know his path of escape if needed. She was like a lioness circling her prey.

She'd batted his first excuse away, so he offered another.

"I didn't know how to ask. Our wedding night had been one thing. An expectation to consummate our vows. But how could I ask for more from a woman who never planned to marry in the first place?"

She shook her head.

"No. You are not a man who would forgo something he wanted because of a bit of awkwardness. You didn't hesitate before. I don't think that is the reason you hesitate now." She took a few steps closer.

He was in danger of telling her everything.

But then he remembered, he had another card to play, so to speak. He had something she wanted. Him. He could distract her by giving her the very thing they both wanted.

It was an easy thing to turn the tables on Thea. To step up, meeting her so their chests touched. He bent to kiss her. No, it wasn't a kiss so much as a claiming of her mouth.

When she was gasping and dazed, he scooped her into his arms and carried her through the private doors between her rooms and his. He set her down in front of his bed and began tugging at their clothes. Now that he'd started down this path, he couldn't wait to lie with her.

He ripped her gown in an effort to unfasten the buttons.

"You are a danger to my wardrobe, my lord."

"I will see you are not forced to walk around the estate na-ked." He paused and then looked at her. "Perhaps I should rethink the situation."

She batted him playfully in the arm and he took the advantage by grasping her arm and kissing the spot of ink that had been tempting him on her wrist. "I do hope I'll not have to replace all my linens having all this ink in my bed."

She laughed again and reached for the falls of his trews. She managed better than she had the first night, but she was still too slow for his liking. After another button, he took over, all the sooner to get to her.

He pulled off one of her stockings and then the next before tugging the ugly dress off of her. And then he stepped back.

"The modiste will receive my thanks for this work of art," he mumbled.

He'd asked for something pretty. Silk and lace. And the woman had delivered. The lace cutouts were strategically placed at certain areas to tempt a man. He could just see the shadow of a pink nipple, and the hint of blond hair lower between her legs.

As lovely as it was though, he found he wanted to rip it from her body like the last one. Some hint of his intentions must have shown in his eyes for she stepped back and held up a scolding finger.

"No you don't, my lord. I love this new shift and I'll not have you ripping it. I will remove it."

"Then hurry."

Fortunately, she did.

They came together with a groan of pleasure as if they'd been away from each other for years instead of a mere week. He was quite proud of his distraction. And perhaps it wouldn't matter this time. If he could just focus on the pleasure of being with her, he shouldn't care what name she cried out.

He rose above her, knowing she'd thought this position the only option initially and he wanted to show her all of them. She looked up at him as he rocked into her and he felt like the god he'd mentioned earlier. Not for the first time he couldn't believe his good fortune.

He shifted so he could touch her in the place that escalated her pleasure. Not that he wanted to rush, but he worried his control was slipping and wanted to see to her first.

Her eyes went wide for a moment when he caressed her and then her gaze focused on him. "Yes, Shay. Yes!" she chanted.

He tried to ignore it. Tried to take in everything else that was happening between them. The heat of their bodies where they touched. The way her pupils seemed to fill in, blocking out the brown. They way her blonde hair was strewn around his pillow. That bit of ink on her wrist.

It was working. When she clung to him and then called out, he was right there on the edge with her. He was able to block out everything but the buzzing in his ears as heat pulsed down his spine and into Thea.

He collapsed next to her, panting for breath, and smiling. Perhaps he'd only needed time to determine a path forward.

But then she curled into him, looked up into his eyes and said, "That was perfect, Shay."

Hearing her say the name he'd claimed for years should not have slammed into his gut like fist from a prizefighter. He'd never blinked an eye when anyone else had said it. Even in the early days at Heriot, hearing his friends call for him with a name that was new and awkward didn't cause this level of discomfort and pain.

His other lovers had used that name. Over and over, quite loudly in fact, and it hadn't bothered him in the slightest.

Why now? Why did hearing her say that name cause such a visceral reaction? Perhaps it was the intimacy they shared when they were in bed together. It was different in every way, including this.

He couldn't fathom how he would survive hearing her say it another day let alone the years that stretched out before them. He couldn't avoid lying with her, this past week had been torture. And he didn't want to avoid her. He wanted her to know him.

There was only one thing to do.

Chapter Twenty-Five

AFTER HAVING DISCUSSED where they would sleep and what activities they would enjoy, things became easier between them. Thea slept in bed with her husband each night, often after a round of lovemaking. One or the other would wake up their partner with kisses or touches that kept them late for their morning meal most days.

And when they were up for the day, Thea spent time in her study writing with her husband sprawled languidly across the settee either reading or sleeping.

On those occasions when he was napping she found herself distracted by him. She would just look at him when he was relaxed and at peace, and in those moments she thought she could see that small boy alone in a world that had planned to corrupt him.

She was so happy he'd been saved and brought home where he belonged.

It was as if everything had worked out for them like a happily ever after in a book. Except…

It seemed living in the brightest sunshine cast a darker shadow over the one part that was not so perfect.

Despite the pleasure they shared in bed, Thea couldn't help but wonder if she was doing something wrong, or if not wrong—

for it seemed an easy thing—then not to Shay's liking at least.

She'd seen him wince, or close his eyes, and not in the way that meant he was overwhelmed with desire. This was different. It looked as if she were causing him actual pain. She'd asked twice if everything was all right and he'd assured her it was. Actually, what he'd said was that he would be all right.

She remembered now that she didn't know if he'd meant the distinction or something being all right or something that *would* be all right. Whatever it was, it was clear he didn't wish to speak of it. And when it had happened, she made sure to note if she was touching him in the same place, but she hadn't.

One time she had her hands rested on his back. Once they had been on his face. Once they hadn't been touching him at all for her fingers were clenched in the pillow. And just this morning she'd had both hands on his buttocks. She'd been squeezing them rather hard so she expected that might have elicited a bit of pain, but he'd not complained until she'd just released him.

It seemed ungrateful for her to worry over this one small thing after having lived in so much turmoil; this thing seemed quite insignificant. But she found herself waiting and wondering when it might happen again so she might solve the mystery of what she was doing wrong.

She put her mind back to her book where it belonged and was into her third page for the day when she saw movement.

"Nay, stop," Shay mumbled from his place on the settee. Since she'd been sleeping with him, she'd come to understand what Mrs. Murray had told her was most true. That her husband was haunted by thoughts from that life.

What horrors he must have seen that they'd embedded themselves so deeply to still hurt him all these years later.

"Wake up. Wake up, Sheamus. You must wake up," he said more clearly than he ever had before.

She stood to go to him. She didn't know if it helped that she woke him, but she couldn't stand to see him so frightened when she had the power to put the end to his terrors.

"Wake up. Please, Sheamus," he repeated the words she was likely going to say to him. At night she only picked out a few random words. Mostly moans. But she'd heard him mention Sheamus before.

She assumed there must have been another boy in his group that had the same name as he. When she'd asked once, he'd just shook his head and changed the subject.

Her curious nature had her devising an entire story about this other boy. She imagined he was likely lost since Shay hadn't the interest to speak of him. Had Shay found the other boy already dead and attempted to rouse him to no avail?

Letting out a breath, she placed a hand on Shay's arm and shook him slightly.

"Nay. Let us be."

"Shay? Wake up. You're having a bad dream. It's Thea. Wake up." With another hearty shake he opened his eyes.

"Shay?" he said, confused, until he blinked and looked around the room. "Thea."

"Yes. I'm sorry. You were dreaming."

He nodded and wiped a hand over his face.

"Perhaps if you talked about it. I think it is supposed to take the power from the specters if you speak of—"

"Nay. I can't. I'm going to go for a ride."

"Would you like me to join you?"

"Nay. You've work to do. I don't want to keep you from it." She knew that meant he'd rather be alone. She nodded and wished him a good ride then went back to her story. But she couldn't help but think of the other Sheamus and how different things might have turned out for him.

SHAY PULLED PHANTOM to a stop on the rise looking down on the castle and the village. There was nothing around for miles but sheep. He felt as if he could scream his secrets and no one would hear. Would doing so free him from his guilt?

He didn't know. What he did know was that the guilt seemed to be getting worse each day he didn't tell Thea the truth. He'd felt the usual guilt at first as he'd felt when he was with Finn or Reese. Lying to people you respected and cared for was daunting. He often wished he could just tell them and be judged. Perhaps they would forgive him in time and he would be set free.

But this despair he felt with Thea was different and he could only think it was because he didn't just care for Thea. He was beginning to feel love for her. Which was terrifying, for he didn't deserve such a thing in return.

How could he love someone and lie to them about his very existence? The two things were at war with one another in his soul and his heart was a casualty.

She'd woken him after he'd been calling for Sheamus. Surely she must have questions. Any person would, but his wife was the curious type and she would take any small fact and create a story around it. What had she put together regarding this story?

He guessed she wasn't even close to the truth, for it was scandalous indeed, and Thea seemed set on thinking the best of him. Even when she shouldn't. If she knew all the things he kept from her, she would surely despise him. That didn't mean he shouldn't do it.

He'd planned to do it days ago, but each time she looked at him he wanted one more day of her looking at him like that. One more day that she thought of him as a good person. One more day that she didn't know the horrible truth.

As if to compound his anxiety, there were actually two things he was keeping from her. One he hoped to resolve promptly so it would not cause an issue.

It left the other secret. Perhaps the biggest, and maybe that would be enough to assuage his guilt so he might find some peace and happiness with her.

He continued to ride until he came to the streets of Inverness.

He rambled about as he sometimes did when he was thinking of the past. And like those other times, he wandered down an alley to a stable behind a brothel where he and other boys like him had spent their nights. Sometimes curling up to a horse to stay warm if the beast weren't especially against it.

A life was lost here. And one taken that didn't belong to him.

He'd never told anyone, but it was time. He couldn't go on like this.

He returned home late, and was not surprised to find the dining room empty.

"Did she eat anything?" Shay asked Mrs. Murray.

"Aye. I had a tray taken to her rooms and then checked in to see that at least some portion of it was gone. She will not waste away, though I should warn you if she is with child she will need to take better care."

A child.

Shay had not considered it, but they'd done nothing to prevent it. And Harrington and the auld marquess would want an heir to pass on the Flemming title someday. Shay had never planned to marry let alone have children, but perhaps the men that had so changed his life were turning things in his favor from beyond the grave.

In her rooms, he paused to watch Thea as he always did. After a few moments, he cleared his throat to get her attention.

"Oh, my. It's late. Forgive my rudeness. When the words are flowing I feel as if I can't stop or they may never return. It's a silly fear as that has never happened, but still I don't wish to risk it."

He smiled and came in to place a kiss on her lips.

"I've just returned home. We've both missed dinner. Would you care to sit and have a drink before going to bed?"

She nodded. "That sounds wonderful. The spirits will help slow my mind so I might sleep rather than lay awake another night thinking over how to conclude this story."

"I didn't realize how much of yourself is given in such an endeavor. I can say a man on the docks doesn't work as hard as you, Thea."

"Well, it is growing to the end. In a few days—maybe a week, I'll write the grandest words of all."

He smiled at her, knowing what they must be. "The end." She would have been done weeks before if not for his constant distractions. That was one of the few things he didn't feel guilty about.

"Yes. It's an amazing feeling when it's finished."

"And then seeing it become a book you can hold in your hand?" He could only imagine the sense of accomplishment at such a thing.

"Yes. That too. The whole process is a labor of love. It's different this time though. It was always something I experienced on my own. I'd never shared it with anyone. The MacLains know enough of the business end of it, but not the more intimate pieces."

"Is it sweeter being able to share it with another person?" he asked, hoping he had not ruined it for her.

"Yes. I think so. There is a certain amount of discomfort too."

"How so?"

"You know a very big secret of mine. I'm…vulnerable. You've said you are an honorable man and will not speak of it with anyone, but in truth we don't know each other all that well despite being married."

"I guess you know me as well as any other person," he admitted.

She tilted her head. "What do you mean by that?"

Leave it to Thea to ask more questions when he'd not wanted to say so much already. He'd made the decision that he needed to tell her the truth, but he hadn't meant today. And certainly not right now. He knew one way to ensure she stopped asking questions he wasn't ready to answer.

He smiled and leaned down to kiss her.

"I didn't mean anything except that even when you think you know someone, they can still surprise you."

He kissed her again and this time he picked her up to carry her off to the closest bed, which was actually the one in the marchioness's bedchamber rather than his bigger bed.

As had become their habit, kissing escalated to the removal of clothes and the touching of bodies. He teased her with soft kisses along her ribs, touching her everywhere, but not the place she needed him most.

It was a game but she soon grew frustrated.

"Please. I need you, Shay," she moaned into his ear and he stilled. Or rather froze solid as the word caught in his mind sending something icy and visceral through his veins. That now-familiar feeling of guilt and shame he'd not felt since he'd been a boy.

She must have felt his body tense for she pulled back to look up at him.

"Shay? What is it? Please tell me."

"It is nothing," he said, his voice cracking. He leaned closer to kiss her again, but she shook her head and pulled away.

"Please. Tell me." Their desire cooled like a hot, iron rod being thrust into icy loch water. He half expected the room to be filled with steam. He might have laughed if he was capable of such a thing.

He tried to swallow back the lump that had lodged in his throat and couldn't seem to speak past it. He was having difficulty even breathing past it.

It had been so long since hearing that name had caused this sort of reaction. All day he'd been thinking of how he would tell her and when, and it seemed it wasn't for him to choose. He'd tried to remain pleasantly distracted. But he couldn't bear hearing that name pass her lips when they were like this together. Each time it felt like a lash against his heart.

It was all a lie. One he'd taken on to survive. He didn't care much that the rest of the world thought he was someone he wasn't. But Thea… Lying to her felt like the gravest offense.

"I need to speak to you about something." He found himself

saying while a voice that sounded very much like his own screamed out for him to remain quiet. Telling her this truth could ruin everything between them. Could very well bring down every broken piece of his life. A life he'd cobbled together with mistruths and guilt.

He'd been lying to everyone for so long, it should have been easy to continue. He was long past worrying that someone would suspect the truth. People wanted to believe what was told to them. Even with rumors and accusations, like those Stephen had brought up, no one could prove anything different.

But in this, with his wife, he couldn't do what was easy or expected. He needed to do what was *right*. Even if it ruined everything. And when he thought of her knowing, he found himself wanting to tell her. So that she'd know *him*. One person who would know who he really was.

"I…" He started but then paused. It was one thing to decide to tell someone and another to find the proper way to do so. He decided to do it the same way he did everything. Straight forward. "I am not the real Sheamus Buchanan."

Thea gasped and he guessed he'd provided quite a twist in his own story.

Chapter Twenty-Six

"I DON'T UNDERSTAND. You are an imposter?" Thea wrapped the linens around her naked body and sat up against the headboard. She knew he hadn't been the late marquess's son, but he was the heir they'd searched for and found living on the streets. Wasn't he?

Her brother had made such an accusation of Shay's lineage when he'd been here. He'd said people spoke of the possibility that Shay was not the real Marquess Flemming, and now it seemed they might be right.

"Only in that I was not born with that name. But I have claimed it longer than the real Sheamus Buchanan." He shook his head. "I think I started in the wrong place."

"It is a common mistake of mystery writers. You should give enough information so that the reader is invested in learning your story."

He smiled at her as if he appreciated her guidance.

"Sheamus Buchanan—the real Sheamus Buchanan—was my best friend. I was on my own at six, and joined up with a gang of three other boys. All of us just trying to survive the streets of Inverness. Sheamus joined a year later and I took a liking to him. We were fast friends. You would've never seen a better pickpocket than Sheamus.

"He told me of his life before ending up on the streets. He'd grown up in a manor house with his parents and a younger sister. When they'd all fallen ill and died, he was to go live with his mother's uncle who he remembered being a mean man. Rather than risk being beaten, he ran away.

"He told stories of his life before. Leaving his dog had been something that made him cry. When things were especially bleak, I would ask him to tell a story of his home so I could imagine a better life where a boy would be called for dinner each night and would be allowed to eat his fill instead of always feeling the pain of hunger in his gut.

"He always rambled on about his home and puddings and toys. He also spoke of his mother and father. I surely never had puddings or toys growing up and I didn't have a father either."

Thea frowned and reached out to put her hand on his. She wished to offer some comfort for the small, hungry boy he'd been.

"The five of us usually made enough to keep our bellies full throughout the summer, but cold weather meant fewer people coming and going on the streets. It meant less food sitting out to be snatched up by hungry lads. It was always worse in the winter months. And winter is long in the Highlands.

"Sheamus fell ill. A bad cough. Then he came down with a fever. The other boys moved on, afraid to get the sickness. But I stayed with my friend, bringing him what food I could find. He became delirious asking me to bring his mother or father. Eventually he fell quiet and I was glad that he was able to fall asleep, but he wasn't asleep."

Shay pressed his lips together for a moment before he swiped at his eyes and cleared his throat.

"Months later, I heard a toff was looking for Sheamus. I found him, thinking to tell him what happened, but instead he thought I was him. We looked similar. Close in age. Same hair color. I asked the man why he was looking for Sheamus. And he said that my great-uncle had fallen ill and wasn't expected to recover and that I was the heir to the marquess."

"And you thought being a marquess sounded better than dying on the street?"

He nodded. "Aye. They asked me the names of my family and even my dog as a confirmation of sorts. I passed their test. The toff was Harrington. He was the great-uncle's companion. After spending time with them at Cawdor… I knew that wasn't exactly true. As a boy living close to a brothel, you see things. Men who have an interest of other men. But this was different. Even as a boy I could see they were in love. I realized quickly why there had been no other heirs. Lord Flemming and Harrington were kind men. And when the marquess died I thought helping me get settled in my duties seemed to help Harrington deal with his loss. So I felt it wasn't so bad what I did."

"This makes you feel guilty?" she asked while stroking his back. She already knew the answer, could feel it in the tension he held in his body.

"I had good reasons for what I did back then. Dozens of them. I was starving and cold, and this old man needed to believe his title would go on. I gave him peace in his final days. But as the years went on, those reasons faded into nothing. There is no reason why I should still be living this lie."

"What would Sheamus Buchanan have thought of all of this?"

He shook his head. "I try not to think of the betrayal to him."

"But was it a betrayal? You cared for him, stayed with him when everyone else left him. You were his friend in a place where friends would stab another in the back for survival." She decided she might need to ask a different question to help her husband. "What if things were reversed. If you were really Sheamus Buchanan and you had died and your friend was likely going to suffer the same fate but for a man showed up looking for you and found him instead. What would you have wanted him to do?"

"I—I…" It was clear in all this time, Shay had never asked that question or thought of it in that way. He'd only thought of what he'd done. What lie he'd told.

"Would you have wanted him to grasp onto that opportunity? No one else would have it. So why not you?"

Shay blinked at her.

"I would have wanted him to be safe. No matter what lie he had to tell. I would have wanted a warm home for him." His eyes glistened. "Thea, do you really think he would have understood and wanted this for me?"

"You knew him best. What do you think?"

IT SEEMED SUCH a simple thing to answer. Yet Shay had not once in all this time considered things from that side. That perhaps Shay—the real Sheamus Buchanan—would have wanted him to claim his birthright so he might have a better life since he couldn't.

It had been too late for him, but good had still come from Sheamus's life. The stories he'd shared.

"What do you think?" Thea asked him again when he'd sat there for a few minutes unable to speak. He wanted to make sure he really knew the answer rather than giving himself some half-true reason to justify what he'd done. And after allowing himself to remember the boy he'd worked hard to push into the shadows of his memories, he had his answer.

"He would have wanted the same for me, Thea. If he could not have been saved, if it had been too late for him he would have wanted it for me. Just as I would have wanted it for him if things had been different."

The relief came swiftly, stealing his air and breaking him down. Suddenly he was that boy again crying for his friend who had not been able to hold on long enough. This time, though he was not alone. Thea held him tight as he wrapped his arms around her waist and sobbed. She consoled him with her hand rubbing circles on his back and her fingers stroking through his hair.

"You did the right thing, uh…" Thea paused then whispered close to his temple. "What is *your* given name?"

He looked up at her allowing her to brush the tears from his cheeks. She wanted to know his name. She wanted to know him.

His lips felt strange making the words, it had been a lifetime since he'd uttered them.

"Ellis." He swallowed and pushed the rest of the name up from his very soul. "My name is Ellis Ballantyne Hayes."

Thea smiled. "It is very nice to make your acquaintance, Ellis Ballentyne Hayes."

Hearing his name on her lips brought more tears to his eyes. He was becoming a watering pot, but he was overcome with emotions he'd not allowed himself for so long.

And now he wasn't alone. Someone knew his secret. Thea knew and accepted him. Had given him peace.

"Thank you," he managed when he pulled himself together.

She shrugged as if her generosity was nothing of note. "As someone who uses a different name for safety, how could I not understand you having done the same thing."

He brushed a lock of golden hair behind her ear and looked into those warm, brown eyes that seemed limitless in their understanding.

"How did I get so lucky as to have you intrude on my life?"

"I'm not certain, but I may have to write a story about it."

He kissed her and since they were still naked, it was an easy thing to pick up where they'd left off. Each touch between them was sweeter for having this burden lifted, this wall felled between them.

He'd never known such peace or joy. Where guilt and worry had been he was now free to be with her as himself.

She was the only living person who knew who he really was, and as she reached for him, with desire in her eyes, she cried *his* name.

"Ellis!"

<hr>

Chapter Twenty-Seven

H ER HUSBAND WAS not the person she'd thought, but he was still the same man. Her heart broke for what he'd endured and the guilt he'd carried all these years. She hoped he could now forgive himself, knowing that anyone would have done the same in that situation.

No one had been harmed by his deception. In fact, many people had been given a better future because of it. The late Lord Flemming had left this world knowing his line would go on. Harrington had likely been happy with the distraction of bringing up a new lord after his love had passed. Shay—or Ellis—had been given a life he would never have had, but one every child deserved. One with security and a chance for a happy future.

And then there was her. She had also been blessed by this man who had offered his protection from an unpleasant fate.

As their touches had turned from comfort to desire, she wanted to give him something she thought he needed. She'd seen the way he'd flinched before and now she realized it was when she'd cried out his name in bed.

When they were intimate and his defenses were down it must have been difficult for him to hear that other name. This time as he kissed along her collarbone and flicked his thumb across her nipple she allowed a different name to flow out of her.

"Ellis," she said on a gasp and he raised his head to look at her with burning blue eyes.

"Say it again," he demanded.

"Ellis, please." She shifted restlessly, needing him so.

She'd only hoped to spare him unease by using the name that wasn't truly his, but she'd unleashed some wild part of him. When he kissed her she felt some freedom she'd never felt before.

This time as they made love there were no secrets between them. And when he looked into her eyes as they found their release they saw each other for who they really were.

"I didn't know I could feel so free. I know I can't tell anyone else for it would ruin many things, but telling you has changed everything, Thea."

"I will keep Shay during the day, but my nights will be shared with Ellis."

He nodded and gave her a happy grin.

They talked, him sharing what his life had been like all this time. The danger and risk. All the worry he'd had at first that he might accidentally give himself away. What a burden for such a young boy.

She wasn't sure if she fell asleep first or he did, but eventually they woke in the late morning.

"It is a new day," he said as he kissed her and got out of bed. "Come. We shouldn't waste a moment of it. I'd like to take a stroll through the gardens if you can delay your writing for just a little while this morning."

"I believe that can be arranged. Since there is no hurry in me having to finish this book now, I will allow a distraction."

She actually welcomed any time she could spend with her husband. She'd never planned to wed for doing so meant giving up herself and everything she had become. But never had she dreamed she could have both.

A husband and her writing.

As they sat, side by side, eating their morning meal, Shay went through the post, stopping on a letter that had pulled the smile from his face.

"What is it?"

He breathed out a resigned sigh. "I'm afraid I'm needed in London to take care of some business."

She nodded, keeping the smile on her face. She would miss him. She knew from her trip here it was near to two weeks to get to London, which meant it would be at the least a month without him, not counting how much time he would need to stay to see to his business.

"Of course."

"Why do you look upset? Buchanan House has a study you can use for your writing. Besides, you'll soon be ready to turn in your manuscript. You might as well do that while we're in London, aye?"

"You wish for me to go with you?" she asked, with some surprise.

"While I do want to see to this situation, it is not enough to take me away from my new bride. I will not go if you do not accompany me."

She smiled. "Then I shall have to do my duty. After all, I am your wife and my place is at your side."

"We shall pack and leave early in the morning."

"I shall be ready," she promised.

Fortunately, her new gowns arrived that afternoon and Frannie was able to see to packing them for their trip. Frannie was nearly beside herself with excitement for she'd never been to London before.

"I will make sure to show you all the best things," Thea promised her maid.

Frannie looked a bit sad and Thea wondered if she would miss her family.

"No, it's not that, my lady. It's just..." The girl shook her head. "Never mind. All is well." But Thea was becoming quite the expert on knowing when someone felt guilty about something and she was all but certain Frannie was hiding something.

Their voyage to London was quite different than what Thea had experienced on her way. No longer was she alone and frightened, worried about what might happen to her, but now she spent most of the ride in the marquess's luxurious carriage talking with him and occasionally doing other things…

While she preferred ink, she took to using a pencil on a traveling desk in the coach so she could continue to write when the urge took over. She was very near to finishing. She would be pleased to turn in the manuscript, but there was none of the urgency she'd felt before.

It was odd being back in London with completely different circumstances. She was a married woman now. One of means. She was able to visit the modiste and the bookstore without anyone looking askance.

She'd even met a few women her age and she and Shay had received invitations to societal events.

Shay was happy to go with her. He was pleasant to their hosts and charming to her new acquaintances. But something was wrong.

He'd taken to spending more and more time in his study alone, instead of sitting with her in the library as she wrote. When he came to bed, it was very late, and more than a few times he'd been out all night long.

She started to wonder if this business he'd spoken of had something to do with a mistress. Not being one to stay quiet she asked him when he came downstairs late the following morning.

"Do you have a mistress?" she said, not sweetening the question in anyway. Like her mysteries she knew a person's reaction to a question often told more than the answer they gave.

Shay's brows came together and he shook his head.

"No. I've never had a mistress. Never needed one for I had invitations from widows. And now, if you haven't heard, I'm a married man, and I'd not betray my vows. Do you truly think I would keep a mistress when I'm married to you?"

"Guilty people often answer a question with another question."

He chuckled, clearly unperturbed by her questioning. That spoke to his innocence.

"No, Thea. I do not have a mistress." He held her gaze as he spoke, something he'd not been able to do previously when he'd lied to her about being all right when he was not.

"I believe you. But you've been out all hours and I do wonder what kind of business is conducted so late at night." She wanted him to confide in her so she might put her worries to rest, but he didn't.

"It's nothing for you to worry about. How is the book coming along?" he asked and she was sure he was attempting to distract her. Her brother had done as much when he started selling off their belongings.

"The book is nearly done. You are falling behind on the pages I've finished."

"I'm sorry. I will have time to catch up after..." He didn't finish his sentence, but she knew better than to ask what he was going to say. Instead, she asked a different question.

"Are you gambling?"

"I—no. I'm not gambling. I would not do that knowing how much it would worry you. But again, I'm not like Stephen. Not all men who gamble are obsessed with it like he is. Do you understand?"

She nodded. She knew that was true. What she didn't know was why he wouldn't just tell her what he was doing. The fact it was a secret made her wary.

She didn't think Shay would lie to her, but he had before.

Chapter Twenty-Eight

S HAY STARED AT the books in front of them while wishing he could grab Barnabas Flint by the neck and give him a good shaking.

The man was making the sale of *Nuit Noire* more difficult than needed. The way it was drawing out was sure to make Thea suspicious. She had already asked him if he had a mistress. Which he did not.

But then she'd asked if he was gambling. Once again, he was able to answer honestly, that he was not. But if she knew he was spending every hour of the night in a gaming hell, she would surely not believe he hadn't been gambling.

Instead, Shay spent the majority of his time in Flint's office trying to negotiate a deal they would both be content with. So far the man was not budging.

"The way you are frowning at those ledgers has me wanting to back away and run far and fast," Reese said as he stepped inside Shay's study. "But because I'm a better friend, I'll at least ask what's wrong first."

Shay rubbed his forehead. "Is it too early in the day for a drink?"

Reese chuckled. "Did ye forget you're a Scot and therefore are permitted to drink whenever ye wish?" Reese went to pour them each a dram of whisky. Shay studied it for a moment before throwing it back.

He knew well the answers to one's problems were rarely found at the bottom of a glass, but for a few moments at least, it would make the burden he was carrying easier to bear.

He'd lied to Thea about everything.

It had been astounding the way she'd accepted that he himself was the biggest lie of all. His name, the very person he'd been pretending to be for most of his life was all a fabrication and she'd only offered understanding and peace.

He knew her well enough by now to know that was the easier of his deceits. This next one would not be so easily forgiven. Not by a woman who still bore the scars of her brother's disease on her soul.

Shay had justified his silence by thinking he was sparing her unpleasantness she didn't need to know about. Especially when he was working to remedy the situation as soon as possible.

But just because he would no longer be doused in incriminations didn't mean it had never been. He'd thought with the business out of his hands he would be free, but the sale had not yet gone through and he already felt the weight of guilt on his shoulders for all he was hiding from a wife he had taken to protect, but had come to love.

One didn't lie to people they loved. It was something he'd heard his mother say before she'd died. A simple truth if there ever was one. And one he had betrayed.

"What is bothering you? Is it the sale? Are you sure you want to do this?" Reese asked, pulling Shay's attention to his current issues.

"You're the one who told me I should sell," Shay pointed out.

"I did, but I didn't think you'd take my advice. You never have before."

That may have been true. In fact, he was not selling *Noire* because Reese suggested it, but because he needed to. To make things right with Thea.

"I'm very sure. I'd like to have it done today if it could be arranged. I just want to be out of the whole business. Then I can put my estates back to rights and move on with my life."

"You know if you need anything, I would—"

"I do know it. Things are not as bad as I'm making them out to be. The financial aspect will be remedied soon enough, but the damage it has already done and the risk it poses…"

"You're worried Lady Flemming will find out?"

He'd told Reese about how his marriage had come to be. And her concerns about gambling.

"Nay. It is worse than that. I'm worried I'll not be brave enough to tell her." For it was becoming clear that he would not just be able to go about things as if he'd not once owned the very gaming hell where her brother had lost a large portion of their money. Likely her dowry was spent at Shay's tables. "How will I live with that, Reese? This thing between us?"

"It is quite common for men to keep things of import from their wives. Women rarely have any knowledge or interest in business affairs anyway. So long as the modiste accounts are kept up, all will be well."

Shay could only laugh.

"The words of an unmarried man."

Reese lifted his glass. "May all my words be as such for the rest of my days."

Shay tilted his head, really inspecting his close friend for the first time.

"I know you hate the mamas and misses hunting you like a prized boar, but do you truly not wish to find a real wife? After seeing how happy Finn has been with Lily and their son? Do you not wonder if it wouldn't be a better life spent with someone you could actually care about and someone who might care about you?"

Unlike the rest of them, Reese still had a living parent. His mother, Dowager Breckenridge, was a meddling woman who wanted Reese to find a wife and start a family. She was not beyond setting up her own trap to comprise her own son into marriage. The woman probably didn't realize that her constant badgering only made her quarry fly harder and faster to elude her.

"Have you found a love match, Shay?" Reese asked, looking at Shay in a similar way as Shay was looking at him. It unnerved Shay to have to look away first, but continuing in this test of wills would show more truth than Shay was comfortable with.

Reese chuckled, while Shay glared at his gloating friend.

"I can't say yet." Only because it didn't seem right to admit such a thing to someone other than Thea first. "I would say there is much I admire about my wife. She is a true friend, and confidant. And then there are the nights." He couldn't help the smug smile that took over his lips.

"You know well a man can have the nights without all the other worrisome bits."

Shay shook his head. "Nay, the nights are much different when there is affection. I'll not attempt to explain it to you for you're not ready to listen. And I admit it does sound like quite a lot of bluster, but one day I hope you find a woman who would be true to you so you might know what it is like."

"A woman who would be true? You may as well wish for me to stumble upon a unicorn."

Reese was surely the most handsome of them and his coffers were full. He was at the top of the list in every drawing room across London as the most eligible, despite his rough upbringing in the wilds of Scotland. Much could be overlooked when one had good looks, charm, and money.

But Reese was not above testing these huntresses of their true intensions. Often acting in the most barbaric ways to see them smile politely and act as if all was well just so they could win him over. And then there were the ones who took more deceitful measures of attempting to lure him into a compromising situation. The poor man needed to be on constant alert for any such subterfuge.

"Then I will hope you find a unicorn as well as happiness."

"I thought us friends. Why would you cast such a curse upon me? Take care of yourself and leave me be," Reese joked.

"Very well, when this business is settled and my accounts are put back to rights, I plan to take Thea home to Cawdor, and enjoy some peace. It is my greatest wish to not have this uncertainty hanging over my head any longer."

"Then I hope everything goes as planned. And this unpleasantness is set behind you as quickly as possible."

SURELY, THEA SHOULD have learned by now not to listen in on other's conversations. But in her defense, the last time she'd done it, it may have very well saved her life. Or at least, spared her from a life not worth living.

And she had not listened to much of the conversation between her husband and Lord Breckenridge. She'd only come up to the study door when Lord Breckenridge was jesting about Shay placing a curse upon him. But she'd heard something after that which had her worried.

She trusted Shay. He'd told her his biggest secret and he'd kept hers. Yet, she felt uneasy hearing about some concern over the finances. Was something wrong? More importantly, could she help?

He'd told her he would never touch her money, and it had gone far to reassuring her. Losing her property—as well as becoming property herself—was the main reason she hadn't ever planned to marry. But now that she cared for Shay, she found keeping their things separated seemed unfair.

Afterall, he had not hesitated to use his money to care for her. To provide a roof over her head and his protection. Shouldn't she do the same if it be in her power to do so? They had married under strained circumstances, but things had changed now. She wanted them to be partners in all things.

But rather than wait until Lord Breckenridge left to ask her husband what was going on, she waited until Shay left on business and sneaked into his study to look around. She fully expected Shay to tell her all was well so not to worry her. Which was why she wanted to learn of their circumstances herself.

She understood, she wouldn't want him to worry about anything if it could be avoided either. Perhaps that was what married people did. Right or wrong, they wished to spare the other even the slightest unpleasantness. Even if the other could provide great comfort if not help to sort out the matter.

If eavesdropping had been deemed unsuitable, casting about in her husband's desk, and going through his ledgers felt far worse. She continued to tell herself it was for the best of reasons. But deep down, she knew it was fear that kept her searching. Because she cared for her husband. No. That wasn't correct. It had grown to be more than caring. Still, below all the happiness she'd found from his touch and the love she'd felt in her heart when he simply offered a tender smile, lay the dank shadows of doubt.

She blamed her brother, which was not surprising for he was guilty of many things. Early on, in the time she thought of as *blind oblivion,* she'd believed everything he'd said. And when collectors began gathering at their doors and Stephen said it was but a misunderstanding, she'd continued to believe. She'd bumbled around far longer than any intelligent person should have before realizing what had been there all along.

There hadn't been any misunderstandings. Her brother had lied to her. It had been the first time she'd felt the foundations of her life tremble. And in the days and weeks that followed, the façade shook free until she could see how grim things truly were.

Rather than wait so long to know what situation had worried her husband, she flipped open another ledger, wondering why he had two. It wasn't uncommon for there to be multiple books for each property, but generally they were kept at that property to be maintained by the steward.

"Nuit Noire?" she whispered, reading the name of the property. He'd not mentioned a property called Dark Night. It seemed an odd name for a home or an estate. Any property in Scotland would surely have been listed in Gaelic rather than French. This made her think of a brothel, or some other sinister business, like a… gaming hell.

Thea shut the book and set it aside as if it were a snake ready to strike, as memories came rushing in. The times when Stephen and Billings had spoken of it being a dark night.

She'd found it odd for all nights were dark. It was rather redundant to use the description. Now she was putting it together. Her husband owned a gaming hell. One where her brother had been a patron, and likely lost much of their funds.

Going back into the drawer where she'd found that ledger she pulled out a small tin box and opened it. Flipping through the vows—so many of the small slips of paper were practically wedged in—she found they were alphabetical. It made it easier to maneuver to Lord Percival.

She covered her mouth with a shaking hand when she saw the sheer number of them and the sums written upon them. How much Stephen owed her husband was staggering. She didn't think it was so much as he owed Flint, but then Shay was a smart man. He wouldn't allow someone to keep racking up debt at his tables when there was no hope of repayment.

It seemed Thea had gotten out of becoming reparations to one lender only to have married a different one. Like an evil weed, doubt began to wind through her body, nearly choking the breath from her. Had this all been done on purpose?

But her brother could not know she would escape to Scotland. To end up at Shay's home. Unless that conversation she'd overheard had been meant for her to hear. Would a man who planned to drug his own sister and give her off to pay his debts be above setting a trap to ensure she covered a different debt?

Tidying up the desk, she left her husband's study on trembling legs. She needed to know the truth, but how if everyone who held the answers were set on lying to her?

She took a few deep breaths and then thought of the heroes in her stories. What would they do to track down the truth?

It seemed it was time to begin an investigation of her own, but rather than fiction, this mystery had very real ramifications.

Chapter Twenty-Nine

WHEN THEA TAPPED on the door to the MacLains' home she was cast back to that day when she'd shown up there running for her life, and they'd helped her acquire a carriage so she could set off for Scotland.

Mr. MacLain opened the door and offered a big smile for her before ushering her and Frannie inside.

"Oh, the missus will be so pleased to see ye, lass. We'd worried over you so. Daph! Come see who has shown up at our door," he shouted louder than would have been needed for the small home. "Our boy is here for a visit as well," he added.

"And how is Robert?"

"Well enough. He's been signed on to be the solicitor for the Westbrook Estate, thanks to ye and you providing him such a fine education."

Anything Thea might have said to that was cut off as Mrs. MacLain came into the room and squealed her excitement.

"'Tis so good to see you healthy, lass. We've worried over ye."

"I am well. In fact, I'm not sure you've heard, but I'm the Marchioness of Flemming now."

All three of the MacLains blinked at Thea.

"You've married?"

"Yes. But not to worry, he knows all about me." Thea cast a glance at Frannie who didn't know quite everything about Thea, but Frannie was busy eyeing Robert and he was… doing the same to Frannie. Interesting.

"Sit. I'll get us tea and biscuits so we can catch up."

"You sit too, Mama. I will see to it so you can speak with Miss Thea—uh, I mean Lady Flemming," Robert winced.

"I'll help you," Frannie offered following after the young man.

"Such a good boy he is," Mr. MacLain said as he led Thea and his wife to a seat in their small drawing room.

"Please tell us what happened after you arrived in Scotland."

"I will, but first I must apologize for any discomfort my brother made for you while he was looking for me. I hope he didn't threaten you or harm you in anyway."

The MacLains looked at each other with matching expressions of confusion.

"Your brother didn't come here looking for you. And we surely never said anything as to where you were that it would have gotten back to him. Why we didn't even share the details with Robert. He knew well enough we helped you out of the city, but he didn't know where you went.

It was Thea's turn to look confused.

"But Stephen showed up at Cawdor Castle. He knew I was there. I worried he'd tortured it out of you and I wouldn't have judged you if you'd told him to save yourselves."

They shook their heads.

"There's nothing that little gnat could have done to me to give up your whereabouts," Mr. MacLain promised.

"Then how did he know?" she wondered to herself even as she knew they didn't have the answers she needed.

Perhaps there was only one person who could tell her the truth of the matter, though she'd hoped to avoid him. Turning to Mrs. MacLain she frowned.

"I wonder if you might accompany me to see my brother. I'm

not willing to subject Frannie to him after she had to protect me from him." Thea wouldn't speak of what had happened to Frannie last year.

"Of course. And Arthur will see us there in case we need him."

Thea chuckled. "I would wager on you any day against my brother, Mrs. MacLain."

Thea explained to Frannie about their outing and Robert agreed rather quickly to stay and keep her company until they'd returned.

"It seems my son has a sweetness for your maid, Lady Flemming," Mrs. MacLain said with a grin.

"I was just noticing that myself. She is a kind young woman. It would please me to see her settled with such a fine man as your Robert. I've no experience with matchmaking, but I'd be curious to give it a try if you are."

They laughed in a somewhat evil way as the carriage pulled up to Percival House. Mr. MacLain helped them down and escorted them to door where he knocked.

"Good lord, even the brass door knocker is gone," Thea whispered to Mrs. MacLain.

After a second loud knock, Thea heard mumbling before the door opened and Stephen stood there himself in the foyer in only his shirtsleeves.

"What do you want?" he asked looking rather bleary-eyed. But his speech had not been slurred, and he didn't reek of gin. So she didn't think he was in his cups.

"I have a few questions for you if you will see me. And then with my answers you and I will never have to see each other ever again."

Stephen shrugged and walked toward his study.

Mrs. MacLain went with her while Mr. MacLain stood by the front door.

"I expected you to be dressed in finer gowns, *marchioness*," he said. That last word had a bit of a sneer to it, but she just ignored him.

"I do not need much."

"That's what people of means say."

"How did you know I was in Scotland?"

He smiled slowly. And then leaned forward resting his arms on her father's desk.

"I will answer your question if first you answer mine. Where did you get all that money to hire a fancy private coach?"

"I owe you nothing, but I will say I earned it myself. Now, tell me who told you I was there?"

He shrugged. "In truth, I don't know. I received a letter."

As if he already knew she wouldn't believe him without seeing proof, he opened a drawer and dug around before pulling out a parchment and handing it over.

Thea unfolded the missive and her gaze went immediately to the bottom to see it had not been signed. Moving to the top she read…

Lord Percival,

I believe you are looking for your sister, Miss Thea Rockledge.
She is staying at Cawdor Castle.

She didn't recognize the writing as Shay's, but that didn't mean he couldn't have written it. Often the villains in her books disguised their handwriting when they were up to something nefarious.

"How much money do you owe my husband, Stephen?"

Mrs. MacLain sucked in a quick breath but said nothing. Thea had not been prepared to ask about her husband's business, but suddenly it seemed very important.

He rolled his eyes. "I didn't realize when you married off I would still need to hear your scolds, sister."

"I am only asking. It is your business, not mine. I have a roof over my head, food in my belly, and a safe place to sleep regardless, so what you do is no longer my concern. Not that you were so very concerned about me. Still, I wish to know."

"He came here the first night you were back in town and told me specifically that I wasn't to speak to you, or even look at you. He made it clear I wasn't to bring up his business. He said he would make it worth my while. I guess he made good on that promise, for instead of being hunted, I was merely forced into service for Flint. To work down the debt I owe him, I'm made to clean up after the hell closes each night. I've become a common servant for a ruthless man. But at least he hasn't pulled a blade across my throat and tossed me into the Thames."

Thea shuddered. Despite not wanting to care what her brother got himself into she was pleased to hear the risk of harm had been resolved. Truthfully some work would do her brother well.

"He negotiated with Flint on your behalf. Why would he do that?"

Stephen looked at Thea as if she were daft.

"Because he thought it would win him favor with you. But how could it if he never mentioned it?"

She had no answer. Unless he hadn't negotiated the labor for her but for himself.

"How much do you owe him?"

"Nothing."

"I saw the vows, Stephen. There is no sense in lying." Perhaps there had been no sense in coming here either.

"I'm not lying. He cleared my debts." He held out his hands and glanced away as if admitting as much caused him shame in some way. Though she didn't think her brother still had the ability to feel shame. This lack of honor in paying his debts impacted him more than offering his sister up apparently.

"When?" she asked, wanting to move this along so she could leave.

"After you married him."

Thea swallowed, but it did nothing to remove the lump in her throat.

Had her husband written to Stephen telling him where she

was so Stephen would come to Scotland looking for her? With no other options, she would have had to marry Shay, giving him full access to her funds. He'd said he would never touch them, but legally her money belonged to him. Just as she herself did.

Had everything between them been a lie?

Chapter Thirty

SHAY RETURNED HOME late in the evening after dinner had already been served and cleared away. He should have known Flint would drag out the proceedings to make it as painful as possible.

He'd wanted to sell *Nuit Noire*, but he'd hoped to find some other buyer willing to take it. Mayhap if Shay had been willing to wait, it might have gone better, but in the end it was done and over now.

Shay no longer owned a gambling establishment. He'd bartered a fair deal for Stephen Rockledge as well. Freeing him of his servitude to Flint.

Unfortunately, the worst part was yet to come. He needed to tell Thea the truth. That would not be an easy thing, but it needed to be done as soon as possible.

Passing over an offer of a late meal, Shay hurried upstairs to his wife's study. Despite his worrisome news, his lips pulled up in a smile of anticipation. He wondered where he might find the adorable smudge of ink she always managed to have somewhere on her person.

But when he opened the door he found it dark inside. Light from the moon filtered in on the messy desk, still strewn with paper, some covered with writing, and others blank, waiting to be filled with the words of a master who wasn't there.

Backing from the room he worried she was ill. For that could be the only reason she wouldn't be rushing to get this book done on time. Hurrying to their bedchamber he found it empty as well. But that offered only a short relief. For the room was not just empty of his wife, but her things were gone from the dressing table as well.

Using the adjoining door to the marchioness's rooms he found her gowns hanging there in the clothes press, and her brush and comb on the dressing table in there. Her books were lined up on the small bookcase in the sitting area.

"What the devil?" he whispered as he returned to the hall, heading back downstairs. Running into Frannie, he stopped.

"Where is my wife?" Shay asked, noticing his voice had taken on a frantic quality.

"In the drawing room, my lord." The maid nodded in the direction of the room as if Shay didn't know where his own drawing room was. But while he did very well know where it was, he was baffled as to why Thea would be there.

Did they have a visitor? It seemed an odd thing at quarter past ten in the evening.

Inside the room, he found Thea sitting on a comfy-looking chair he didn't remember having. She was dressed neatly and her hair arranged in a proper coiffure. No golden curls had been given the opportunity of escape. And her face was free of ink smudges.

If it weren't clearly his wife, he would have worried he'd stumbled into the wrong townhome. But it was definitely Thea sitting there pulling rose-colored thread through a piece of linen over and over. It took much too long to put the name to the action for he'd not once seen her do it.

Embroidery.

His wife, writer of dozens of novels with one due imminently, was sitting calmly on a chair embroidering instead of writing. Unless...

"Thea?"

She looked up, and he noted the lack of any expression on her face. She was not happy to see him, yet she didn't seem irritated or angry either. She just… was. Like an automaton that moved in the way of a real person but lacked the spark of emotion.

"Have you finished the book?" he pushed, thinking that could be the only reason for her to have ceased working. He would argue it still didn't make sense that she'd be here embroidering like a proper noblewoman, but he would begin with the simplest explanation.

Her answer was brief. A shake of her head and a flat, "No" before she returned her attention to her work. He stepped closer and noted she was quite skilled in creating a running chain of roses along the edge of some undetermined white linen. But why?

"Thea?" he tried again, his voice lower. This caused an impact.

Her hands stilled, her eyes closed, and her head dropped ever so slightly, but he felt the burden of sadness weighing her down.

Kneeling in front of her he took her hand in his.

"What has happened? What is wrong? Is the book not going well?"

Rather than answer she asked her own question. One that near to gutted him.

"Did the sale of your gaming den go well?"

"You know?"

"About *Nuit Noire*? Yes. I know about that and a great deal of other things."

Bloody hell, had he wanted her to show emotion a moment ago? It was practically flaring from her now, like flames from the windows of a house that had been completely engulfed. She was a raging inferno.

"I know that you allowed my brother to run up huge accounts at your establishment."

"Yes. But I cut him off, hoping to make him stop. It only forced him to go to Flint where he was able to get more credit than was reasonable."

"But he started at *Nuit Noire*, yes?"

He let out a breath, but would only allow the truth to pass his lips. Damning as it might be.

"Aye. Some others as well. But, yes. I gave him credit."

"Which you forgave after we were wed," she added as if this had some great significance.

Shay nodded. "Yes. It seemed the right thing to do." The lad was now Shay's brother by marriage, and while Thea had wanted to pretend she didn't care about the blighter, Shay knew it would not be so easy. Besides all of that, it wasn't as if the man was ever going to be able to pay it back. So writing off the debt was no different than carrying it. Either way, he was out the blunt.

"You paid the debt to Flint, as well."

He shook his head. "Not all of it. I didn't have enough to take on that debt comfortably. As it was, things were a bit tight until *Noire* sold today to refill my coffers. But I assure you everything is fine now. There's no reason to worry."

That had clearly been the wrong thing to say.

Tossing her needlework to the side she stood, fists clenched at her sides.

"No. I imagine there is no reason to worry, is there? You wrote to my brother telling him I was at Cawdor House so he would come there. Then you so gallantly offered marriage. Something I had never wished to do. To lose control of my finances. But now you have all my funds to do with as you wish."

Shay stood there staring at her for a moment. He could not comprehend what kind of trap he had stepped into. She had everything wrong, but all the pieces fit perfectly together. Almost like one of her mysteries.

Except at the end of the book all would not be well for the characters for this was his life and his wife thought him capable of the worst kind of treachery.

But why wouldn't she? She knew the other deceit he was capable of.

"Thea, that's not—"

"I don't wish to discuss it. You may have been compensated, but you'll get not another cent from me. I'm finished writing. I wish to return to the country. Either Cawdor, or another home you have that you never visit. So I will not have to look at you and be reminded of your betrayal."

Shay wanted to explain. To fight back and make her listen, but seeing the tears rolling down his wife's face to drip off her chin, held his tongue. She was angry and he imagined she'd been tied up in all of these tangled thoughts for most of the day.

"I am guilty of many things. Things I had planned to tell you tonight when I got home, which as I say it I know my timing seems suspect. But I did not write to your brother to tell him you were at Cawdor, and I didn't marry you as some scheme or reparations."

She swiped the tears from her cheeks and he stepped forward wanting to comfort her, but she quickly jerked back.

"Very well. It's late. We should get some rest and in the morning, you and I will discuss things through. And if after hearing what I have to say, you still wish to leave for the country, I will make the accommodations as you wish. But know this, Thea. Not everything is a twist of a plot like in one of your books. Sometimes it's just a man who doesn't know the first thing about love, who's trying to do the right thing for someone he desperately wants to love."

She pressed her lips together tightly and he used the silence to say one last thing.

"I didn't trick you into marrying me. I only wanted to protect you. But I'll not lie and say I wouldn't thank the person who facilitated those events. If not for the risk to you, I never would have felt myself worthy of asking for your hand."

He did step closer then, to place a kiss on her forehead before he quit the room and went straight for his study and the whisky. It would be a long night indeed.

He didn't know why he'd thought he could have this. Have her. He had known by now that he was best on his own.

Everyone he'd ever cared for had left him in some way.

His mother was the first. She'd died and while she'd left him in the care of his aunt, it hadn't been long before Deborah had grown tired of caring for a child and left him alone.

The boys had left him when he'd taken on the tending of Sheamus, and then Sheamus himself had gone on, leaving him alone. The auld marquess, and Harrington had left him alone as well.

And now Thea wanted to leave him. He should have expected as much. Nothing good ever lasted. Not for him. It was the punishment he was to bear for all his crimes.

Chapter Thirty-One

T HEA'S MIND SWIRLED with thoughts as if a wind had caught up a full manuscript and tossed it's pages about the room. Chaos and thoughts over thoughts made her grasp the sides of her head and moan.

She tossed again trying to get comfortable in this smaller bed in this too-elaborately floral room she'd never spent much time in before.

She wanted to lie next to her husband, but he was a liar. She'd known that for some time, but what she didn't know was if he were lying about everything or just the things he'd already confessed.

It had not been so long ago she'd stared into her brother's eyes as he'd promised her everything was well even as the servants were let go and the silver had suddenly disappeared.

She knew how easy it was for some people to tell a lie while looking another person dead in the eye. And not show the slightest bit of remorse for it.

But punishing Shay for her brother's crimes was unfair.

And had Shay implied he was in love with her? In all the jumbled ramblings in her head, somehow that one had slipped through until that moment.

She sat up straight in bed.

"Sometimes it's just a man who doesn't know the first thing about love, who's trying to do the right thing for someone he desperately wants to love."

If he were lying, he was quite good at it, for those words had warmed her heart and done much to calm her angry blood. She lay there thinking about what she wanted to stay until the sun came up. Then she decided to go find him so they could get to the bottom of things.

Using the door between their rooms she stepped into the chamber she'd shared with him, only to find it empty and the bed untouched. She sighed knowing she was more likely to find him in his study.

She left their room in search of the man, only to find Frannie huddled outside her room crying.

"Frannie? What is wrong?" Thea helped her to stand, and put her arm around the trembling girl.

"I'm so sorry. I've done something terrible. You're sure to hate me for it."

"Shh. It seems as if a lot of people think I'm to jump to hating everyone. I'm beginning to think I must be some awful ogre."

If Thea thought her jest would ease Frannie's tears, she had been quite wrong. Something else that was happening with increasing frequency.

"Just tell me what has happened and we'll go from there." Better to head straight in.

"I—I sent a letter to your brother, telling him you were staying at Cawdor."

Of all the things Thea thought the girl might say, it was certainly not that. Not just because Frannie seemed too innocent for any such duplicity, but that she obviously hated Stephen Rockledge more than any living person on Earth.

"Whyever would you do such a thing?" Thea asked and refrained from shaking the answer from the girl when she broke down into hysterical sobs.

Eventually she managed to speak again.

"I hated him so much for what he'd done. I thought he loved me, but it was all a lie. I felt like such a fool, which only made me hate him more. I knew the marquess fancied you. If your brother came to take ye away, there would be a skirmish and the marquess would win. I'd wanted to do it myself. I'd wanted to beat him bloody with the fireplace poker, but when the time came, I lacked the strength to see it done."

As reasons went, Thea didn't find this one lacking in much. It did work out as she'd wished. Stephen had gotten a good knocking out of it. Still it had repercussions that far outweighed revenge.

"I'm sorry I didn't realize that he would have thought to protect you by marrying you. Even still, after it was done, the two of you seemed happy enough for a while. But now I see how miserable you are in this marriage and I know it is my fault. I'm so sorry."

Thea let out a breath and brushed back the girl's hair. She should be horribly angry at the maid for interfering. Had Shay not married her she would have faced a life unfit of thinking about. But he had married her. To save her. And he'd told her he had no regrets about it.

She realized she had no regrets either. Perhaps that is why it was so easy to forgive the woman for her foolish plan.

"The truth is, I'm not so miserable in this marriage at all. The marquess lied to me about a few things. I was angry with him, but I realized that I wanted to believe him, because I want to be happy with him."

"So you will not move away to the country? We'll stay in London?"

"I didn't say that. I've about had my fill of London, but when I return to the country, it will be with the marquess. I was on my way to tell him so right now."

The girl smiled, but was not as pleased as Thea expected.

"You do not wish to return home to the country?" Thea guessed.

"I am enjoying the city," she said, but didn't look at Thea.

"Ah. Are you enjoying the city, or are you enjoying Robert MacLain?"

Frannie gasped but then broke into a sad smile when Thea chuckled.

"Is it so obvious? You must think me the biggest of ninnies to have been fooled so completely by your brother only to fall moony for another man. Perhaps my ma is right and I am a danger to myself."

"Perhaps living through such an ordeal is not about never trusting another man ever again, but to learn whom we can and cannot trust. Afterall, not everyone would lie like my brother. And not everyone would be so kind as Robert or Shay. The skill to determine the difference may be the best we can hope for."

"Do you think it is safe to trust Robert?"

"Has he tried to do any—"

"No! We have only talked. Even on the occasion we were alone he never once tried to do anything untoward. Even if he did glance at my lips and stumble over his words a bit." Frannie smiled at the knowledge she'd left poor Robert unsettled.

Thea found herself smiling as well. Women did not hold much power in Society, but that wasn't to say they had nothing to their advantage.

"I should thank you for your part in my marriage to Shay. I think it is time for he and I to work things out between us once and for all."

She left Frannie to go find her husband. She'd made up her mind before her run-in with Frannie, but it was all the more important now that she apologize to Shay for thinking the worst of him.

Thea found her feet moving quickly as she headed for her husband's study. She wanted to know everything about the situation. No more secrets.

She tapped twice on the door before entering, but two steps into the room she wished she'd stayed outside.

SHAY LIFTED HIS thumping head and squinted across the room at the door where Thea stood looking around in dismay. He looked around as well, and had to agree. Things looked rather grim.

In a fit of rage at himself and his stupidity, he'd tossed about a few pieces of furniture. It had felt good at the time to get his frustrations out, but in the light—extremely bright light, as it were—of morning, he had regrets.

Thea spun back for the door, but just as he was about to beg her to stay and hear him out, he heard her speaking to Mrs. Smith, their housekeeper here.

"Please bring coffee for Lord Flemming, and a bit of bread and honey."

That actually sounded like the most perfect thing ever.

A moan from the other side of his desk caught their attention and Shay turned to find Reese had fallen asleep in the corner of the room.

Shay nudged him with his foot.

"Get up, Reese. Time to go."

"But I promised I'd not leave you until you'd won your love's heart. Have you won it, Shay?"

"I'm not certain as of yet, but you're not helping me with your drunken yammering so get up and go."

Shay thought he saw Thea smirking as she turned again for the door.

"Please have Lord Breckenridge's carriage brought around and have one of our footmen see him home and into his bed safely. It wouldn't do for something to happen to the earl."

"Right away, my lady," Markel, the butler, agreed as Reese stumbled to his feet before swaying.

"Good luck to ye, lad. I hope you get her back."

Shay squeezed his eyes closed and rubbed his forehead as a footman came in and escorted Reese out of the room. The door was no sooner closed than it opened again and in came Mrs. Smith with the food Thea had ordered brought in for him.

Thea took the tray herself and carried it over to his desk as the housekeeper left the room.

"Can you eat a bit? You'll feel better with something in your stomach."

"I don't deserve to feel better, Thea. Look at me." He gestured at the rumpled clothes she surely recognized as the ones he'd been wearing the evening before. He reeked of whisky and could barely keep his eyes open for squinting through the blinding light of morning.

"It looks like you had an exciting evening." Again she looked around the room.

"Exciting? Nay." He shook his head.

"What happened?"

"I can't very well give myself a thrashing, so I took out the anger with myself on the furniture."

"And that made you feel better, did it?"

"Actually it did. For a little while at least. Then I made the unfortunate mistake of sending for Reese, hoping he might have advice so I might navigate the treacherous waters I find myself in with regards to a happy future. Why would a married man seek counsel of a bachelor? It doesn't stand to reason at all, does it? But then that was only one more mistake of dozens I've made so far."

She let out a breath and turned the side table back to its feet before sliding it closer to the settee. She took the tray and rested it on the table before holding out a hand to him.

He nearly wept at the touch of her soft, warm hand in his. It was the perfect fit to his larger grip. He'd thought before that she'd been made for him. It seemed true in every way now.

"I'm sorry I kept things from you, Thea. I shouldn't have. I can say I wished to protect you from unpleasantness, but that is not for me to decide. And it would be untrue. I kept it from you so you would not think unfavorably of me."

"But you have shared other things with me."

"Yes. What I did as a boy weighs me with guilt over what I did, but this... running a gaming hell, taking advantage of your brother..." He shook his head. "Guilt is felt for something a person has done. Shame, however, is what a person feels about themselves. When something about them is simply...wrong. That is why it was different. I'm ashamed of what I did. And I am terrified to have you think of me like that. It is easy to forgive a starving boy for doing what he felt he had to in order to survive. But there is no excuse for what I've done."

"Tell me everything. Tell me the truth. And I promise to believe you."

He looked up, unable to hide his surprise. Why would she listen? Why would she believe anything he said? He desperately wanted to pull her to him and ply her with kisses until she forgot he was the villain in this tale. But when the haze lifted, the truth would remain.

He owed her the truth. He owed her so much more than that, but he would give her this and hope she stayed so he might give her everything.

When he still remained silent, she cleared her throat and fidgeted.

"You asked me for a chance. Before I run away to the country and give up whatever we could have together, this is that chance. Do not waste it."

He nodded and searched for the words and the courage to get through this conversation.

Chapter Thirty-Two

THEA WAS IN awe of how clearly Shay understood the differences in one's behavior, specifically guilt and shame. But she also knew how often he'd said he didn't deserve things such as love and happiness.

It seemed to Thea that a man who truly believed he could not have either would have less reason to try. Like a child who is punished when they have done nothing wrong, it would not be long before they would learn it makes no difference if they behaved. If the punishment inflicted was the same regardless, why not just do what one wished?

She thought her husband may have fallen into this trap and by the time he realized he wanted to be good enough for something real, he felt it was too late.

"It is not too late for you, Ellis."

Hearing his real name had an intense effect. He slumped to the settee letting his head hang low with his arms resting on his knees. After a few moments he raised his head and began speaking.

"Very well. The truth, Thea. Everything." With a nod he stood and began to pace the room. "I bought *Nuit Noire*, as soon as I was old enough to order my solicitor to spend the funds. I lived every day in the fear that someone would eventually learn my secret and I would be cast out of all my fine homes and everything entailed would be taken away. I needed something that was not entailed. Something that would earn money so I would never find myself out on the streets like I had been."

She might have asked why it had to be a gaming hell, but if someone wanted to make a great deal of money quickly, it made sense that he would choose such a business.

"Later, as the years went on, and my business became a success, I didn't worry about being found out as much as I had. People talked and cast speculations, but no one challenged me and I began to feel safe. But I still wasn't able to sell it. For whatever reason." He shook his head. "At first, it was a lark when your brother came to *Nuit Noire*. He seemed like any other dandy of the *ton*, with money to spare. Having grown up the way I did, I found his ilk repulsive. And taking their money seemed justified in some way. For now that I didn't worry about surviving, the funds I collected at my tables were shared with those lost children from the streets. I couldn't change what I'd done, but I could use that place to make things easier for those Society chooses to ignore."

When he sat again, she took the seat next to him and placed her hand over his, hoping to help him purge all this pain.

"Your brother is truly the worst player I've ever seen. But beyond his lack of any skill or strategy, he cannot stop playing until he's lost everything. Even when he wins, he plays until his winnings are gone. I'm embarrassed to say it took much too long for me to realize his hunger for the gaming tables was as serious as it was. And perhaps it hadn't been as bad at first. I wonder if I'd turned him away earlier if he might have been spared, or would he have just gotten tangled up with Flint sooner?"

She saw the guilt over this etched on Shay's face, and gave his fingers the slightest squeeze.

"I do not allow my customers to wager too deeply. Even so, Stephen managed to rack up two thousand pounds of debt with the house when I cut him off. He owed others personally as well.

Even Reese was due a hundred pounds. Billings asked me to send him away but I had already seen how bad he'd gotten by then and had instructed my men to keep him out."

"And then he was forced to go to Flint?"

"Aye. Mayhap I should have allowed him to stay. At least with me he wouldn't have been in danger. But I have people who were counting on me for their livelihood. The children. The ladies who served the men."

With this revelation his gaze flicked to her. She made sure to remain still and not show any judgment. Though the idea sickened her, she knew from her research that when a woman had no other means but to turn to that profession the best she could hope for was protection from a fair employer.

Shay had grown up on the streets. There was a chance his mother was in a similar way so of course he would have seen those ladies cared for properly.

She swallowed and he went on.

"I also thought Flint's threats might have scared him straight. But after a beating he showed up at my tables again declaring he was paid up with Flint and ready to make good at *Noir*."

"When I paid them the first time."

"Aye. But I didn't know that then. I did worry he'd done something foolish and the money he was using to clear his debt would be found to be dirty so I refused him. Unfortunately, he continued on with Flint until he got in so deep, he couldn't get out."

She nodded so he would know she would rather skip over the part where her own brother had planned to hand her off to pay his debts.

"And then we married," she prompted the jump in the story.

"I didn't contact him. I would have allowed ye to stay in the cottage all your days."

She forgot he hadn't heard what happened with Frannie and quickly filled him in on those details.

"When we came to London, I met with your brother for a

few reasons. I wanted to make sure he didn't get it in his head to do something to hurt you. Guilt is suffocating, and some men will do anything they can to relieve it. Even worse things than what they'd done originally. I needed to make sure he wasn't a danger to you."

He rubbed his forehead.

"I found out he'd been forced into service with Flint to pay down his debt. I knew I wanted to get out of the business and made an offer to Flint to buy *Noir*. Under the conditions that he forgive Stephen's debt, he never allowed him to play again, *and* that he kept up with taking care of the people counting on the profits from the business."

Thea frowned thinking it sounded like a very gentlemanly arrangement for someone like Flint.

"You think he will keep that bargain?"

"Flint is what he is, but he grew up on the streets same as me. He doesn't have a problem paying back to make others more comfortable. We may have run in different cities. But London or Inverness, a person never forgets what a hungry belly feels like."

She nodded. The fact that Stephen had been put to work rather than tossed in the Thames was a testament to the fact that Flint had some small amount of honor, at least. Perhaps more than her brother.

"I thought if I waited to tell you all of this until after I was done with it, that somehow it would be better. Maybe easier for you to accept. But I realize now as I'm telling you all of this, the timing is irrelevant. I still caused you such pain, Thea. I didn't know you existed at the time, and I didn't trick you into marriage to cover your brother's debt, but I am far from innocent. Your life was destroyed because of me."

"Then it seems only right, that my life has also been fulfilled because of you, does it not? Before my escape from London I lived an imaginary life through my writing. But you have given me a real life. Real happiness. Real hope. Real…love."

His head snapped up as he looked at her intently. Had she

misunderstood what he'd said before? She was sure he loved her as she did him. He'd said he was a man trying to love.

"Love?" he asked, his voice barely a whisper.

Her courage wavered and she glanced away from his piercing gaze.

"That is, I love you, Ellis."

His eyes glistened as he stared at her. Then he took a step forward.

"You love me? After everything you know about me?"

"I love you *because* of everything I know about you."

"And you're sure you're well? You didn't take a turn on the stairs this morning? Because last night I was certain I would be sending you off never to see you again. And now—"

She leaned up on her toes to press a kiss to his lips. She'd meant only to stop his rambling and prove she was of sound mind, but as often happened when their lips met, he wrapped his arms around her and pulled her closer so he could kiss her thoroughly.

When they broke away only far enough to catch their breath, he looked at her and smiled. And that small smile ignited into the brightest grin she'd ever seen on his face.

"Should I ask after your head?" she said when he broke into laughter.

"Perhaps, but not about this. I feel… I feel as if I've been forgiven of my crimes. Ever since that day I lied to Harrington, so I could come here and live this life that wasn't mine, I never felt I deserved anything good. But somewhere someone must have forgiven me, for I never would have found you otherwise."

"Destiny is when the path you were on meets up with the path you were meant to take," she repeated what he'd been told as a child.

He nodded.

"I love you, Thea. I couldn't love you as much as I do without first allowing myself to be loved. I see that now."

"And you'll allow me to love you for the rest of our lives?"

He pressed a kiss to her lips before saying, "I might well demand it."

She smacked his shoulder playfully. "Now you are just being bossy and you know how I feel about that."

"Let me take you upstairs to beg your forgiveness."

Before she could answer, he whisked her up into his arms and carried her out of the study toward their bedchamber.

Chapter Thirty-Three

S HAY COULDN'T BELIEVE his life had turned out like this. Even months since that day when his wife somehow forgave him for all his faults, he still couldn't believe his luck. To have someone like her love him meant he couldn't have been all that bad.

"I have a gift for you," she said after dinner and nodded to one of the footmen to bring it in.

Shay took the bound package and tugged the twine loose so to unwrap it. The cool embossed leather in his palm, brought a smile to his face as he read proudly.

"*The Case of the Golden Feather* by Theodore Stonecliff." He tapped the cover. "I've heard he's quite good." This earned a roll of the eyes from his wife.

He'd read the whole thing already. Page by page as it had been written. The words in this book had brought them together. But he opened it to the first page anyway, excited to see it in print.

But the opening lines were different than they'd been when he'd read it so many months ago.

"*Ellis Ballantyne Hayes stepped out of the carriage in Cheapside and frowned,*" he read. "It seems the hero has a name." It was his name. The name only she called him when they were alone. "Am

I conceited to think this means I am your hero?"

Thea glanced around the room at the servants but her lips pulled up on one side.

"Please give us the room," he said loudly and at his command everyone scattered for the door, leaving him alone with his wife.

"I would think it's safe to say you are my hero."

"As well as your biggest admirer," he added leaning closer to kiss her neck just below her ear.

"I did feel rather admired last night." Her cheeks turned the prettiest shade of pink. Even after all they'd done in bed, she still blushed and it amused him.

In truth, he'd been admiring her with great thoroughness since the day she'd told him she loved him. He simply could not get enough of her, and she had not complained.

It had delayed the completion of the book but another week at least.

"Thank you for the kind gesture, Thea."

"Well, I did think Ellis Hayes should have his moment to shine after all this time. And now he can never be forgotten."

He was touched by her thoughtfulness. It was sad to know that no one had ever noticed or cared that Ellis Hayes just stopped existing all those years ago. If he'd not been found by Harrington and given this new name and new life, he wouldn't have mattered at all. For that reason he always tried to make the world a better place for Sheamus Buchanan having been here.

"Thank you, Thea. I am truly touched."

And since he'd already sent everyone out of the room he took advantage of the privacy and thanked her right there on the table.

THEA HAD BEEN nervous the whole day. More excited than nervous. She only wanted to wait until the right time to tell Shay her news. Their news. She thought he would be pleased to be a father. But she also knew there would be some guilt to traverse.

He'd told her how much it had bothered him to have to give her a name that was not his own. And she guessed that concern would be the same with their child as well. Especially if she bore them a son. An heir to a title Shay didn't feel he owned.

But truly she thought he had to be the best man who ever held the Flemming name, noble blood or not.

After the sale of his business, and the increased sales of her books, she'd asked him to help her do what he'd done. To use the funds from her books to help the children who lived on the streets. Thanks to the proceeds, they were even able to purchase a home for these children. A place where they could be fed and have a safe place to sleep as well as where they might learn a skill that could help them obtain work when they were old enough.

He'd not liked the name she'd picked, but she'd insisted on Ellis House. For her husband deserved to be noted for who he really was, even if no one else understood.

The following month another home would be opening in Inverness for children there. It may have been her emotions with her condition but any time she thought of how Sheamus Buchanan had died, her eyes welled with tears because it could have been her husband who had been lost.

"I have news," she said when the meal had been cleared away and they were walking to his study where he would read to her.

"Is it good news?"

"I think so. No. I'm sure it is." She was ready to blurt it out right there in the hallway, but the butler stepped up, interrupting her.

"Excuse me, but Mr. Robert MacLain is here to see you. He says it is urgent."

Thea felt unease twist in her stomach as they changed course for the drawing room instead of the study. Robert stood and bowed in greeting.

"Pardon for the late visit."

"What is it, Robert. Is something wrong with my new contract?"

She had just signed on for a new book that would be due next year. Giving her plenty of time with the other changes that would be coming in her life.

"No. The contract was finalized this afternoon. Your copies will be coming in the next day or so. This is another matter." He shook his head. "Someone came to my office an hour ago and said it was imperative that they speak to the author of *The Golden Feather*. I told him it was not possible, but any letters of appreciation could be sent to the publisher and would be forwarded to the author as is our arrangement."

Thea did so love hearing from readers about her books. She often wondered if they would be so enamored with her work if they found out she was a woman. Fortunately, there was no reason anyone would ever need to find out. She trusted Robert and now her husband also served as another barrier between Thea and the world.

"But the man said it was urgent that he speak to the author themself. A matter of life and death, he said. I will surely tell him to write if that is what you wish, but I wanted to convey his insistence. I did not feel it was a ruse."

"Life or death? What could make my book so important? It's a work of fiction. Nothing more."

"How do you wish to proceed?" Robert asked.

Thea turned to Shay who was simply waiting for her to decide. She appreciated that he allowed her to run her business on her own in the way she saw fit, except for times such as these when she wished someone else would make the more difficult decisions.

"They asked that I have the author sent to Glenlivet House immediately. That time was of the essence."

"The Duke of Glenlivet," Shay explained. "I've never met him, but I've heard nothing of his reputation that would offer any clues as to why he might want to see you."

"Well, I can't very well ignore something that is life or death, can I?"

Shay grinned. "The curiosity would surely wear away at you."

He knew her too well.

"Let's go. We will not tell them I am the author. We'll let them think it is you," she said to Shay.

"I am honored, wife. So long as I'm not called on to use any complex vocabulary, for we be found out immediately."

She appreciated his jest but as they bumped about the street on the way to Glenlivet House, Thea became nervous again.

"While we have a moment to ourselves, did you want to tell me your news?"

"My news?" she said, forgetting for a moment how their evening had intended to go.

"Yes. I believe you were going to tell me we were going to be parents in a matter of months."

She smacked his arm. "You are awful. You've ruined the whole thing."

He laughed and she joined him.

"Are you happy?" she asked.

"I am thrilled, Thea. So long as you and our child are safe and happy I will be beyond joyous. How do you feel?"

"At the moment I feel nervous, but it has nothing to do with being with child."

"If you don't want to speak to the duke, we don't have to. You have only to say the word and we'll return home and spend the evening celebrating properly."

She shook her head. "I must see it through. I feel 'a matter of life and death' must be dramatic, but what if it truly is that dire and I ignore something so important?"

"Well, you don't have long to wait. We have arrived."

Shay jumped out of the carriage himself and reached up to help her down. She noticed he took extra care to make sure she didn't feel the slightest impact. No doubt this would be the way of things until their child was born.

Shay cared for the people he loved. She surely wouldn't begrudge him that.

Glenlivet House was outdated and gloomy, but they were shown to a drawing room which was comfortable despite the lack of cheer. After a quarter of an hour had passed, Shay stood.

"They call us here and then make us wait?"

She might have offered words of deflection except she was growing impatient as well. Some people had happy news to celebrate with their husband and wanted to get on with it.

A few minutes later as Shay was suggesting they leave, when a man stepped into the room. Not the duke, but a servant.

"I apologize for the wait, but there's been some confu—oh, my." He stopped and stared at Shay.

"I would argue there is much confusion rather than some. Why have we been summoned here and kept waiting?" Shay asked.

The man could only blink and continue staring.

Shay snapped his fingers at the man to get his attention back.

"Apologies. There is much to discuss." He looked around the room and then turned for the door. "Would you please follow me. I think I know how best to explain."

"Are you certain you don't want to return home?" Shay asked.

"Let us not turn back now. Our heroes must see the adventure through."

Chapter Thirty-Four

SHAY WASN'T CERTAIN about seeing any adventure through. What he was, was growing unsettled by all the mystery. Could the little man leading them deeper into the house not just get on with it and tell them why he'd sent for them.

No. He'd sent for Thea. But there was no way he would leave Thea alone for a moment in this dungeon of a house. Everything was dark and either black or a sickly green, it seemed. Only every other sconce was lit which didn't help with the feeling of gloom. Not to mention the stale odor of disuse, or coffins. He couldn't be sure.

They passed another closed door before the man opened the next door and went inside holding it for them to enter. This room was better lit and dare he say, not so depressing. The walls were painted a warm blue and they seemed full of paintings surrounded by rows of books. The library.

Shay looked about for a shelf dedicated to the works of Theodore Stonecliff, or perhaps a pile of them on a desk somewhere, but saw nothing.

"I'm sorry I've been so rude. It's just that the duke is quite ill and well, I've been with him for many years and didn't wish for him to be toyed with or lose hope once again. I am Forney, and, well, I do believe you are not really the Marquess of Flemming."

Shay felt his stomach plummet to his feet. He'd been found out. He knew there had always been a risk and he wouldn't have argued. But now he had a wife and a child on the way.

That familiar desperation from years on the street seared through his blood once again. Whatever proof they had, he would fight it in the House of Lords. He would not allow his family to become destitute because of his mistake.

But as he was working up a powerful defense, his wife tugged on his arm.

He turned to Thea to assure her he would see her provided for but she seemed to be in a trance, staring up at the wall.

Shay turned to see what had captivated her attention so thoroughly and found himself captured by the painting hanging there.

A painting of him.

But of course it wasn't a painting of him. It couldn't be. But the likeness was uncanny. Beside the man was a woman who looked so familiar and in her arms was a bundle of linens. A baby.

He stared at the woman again, trying to figure out where he'd seen her before. At a ball or a musicale possibly. Perhaps she was older now and that was why he couldn't puzzle it out.

But then his gaze caught on the ring on her hand. A pearl locked inside a knot. The very ring Thea wore on her finger now.

"I believe I need to sit down," Shay said as the room began spinning around him. He'd never swooned in his life, even while faint with hunger, but he worried he might lose his feet now.

A chair was brought over and Thea helped him sit, rubbing small circles on his back. "I do believe this mystery has taken an abrupt turn," she whispered.

He might have laughed if he wasn't so far beyond the ability to do so.

"That is my mother, Thea. The ring." He pointed to her finger as he continued to whisper.

"The man in that painting is undoubtedly your father. For he looks exactly like you." Turning to Forney she took charge. "Who is this? When was it painted?"

Forney nodded once.

"This is the Duke of Glenlivet. It was commissioned some thirty years ago, after the birth of his son and heir, Ellis Ballantyne Hayes, Earl of Ainsley."

"Dear God," Thea whispered.

"You may take the chair, for I plan to just fall out onto the floor," Shay said. But Thea was better suited for this than he.

"Is the duke still…"

"Yes. He lives, though he is in grave health. One of the things he enjoys is my reading to him each night. He particularly likes the writing of Stonecliff, and when I purchased the newest book and read the first page we both just sat there. The coincidence was too great. He has been looking for you for twenty-eight years, my lord. And then to just see your name there on the page, it was a shock."

"Yes. It surely is." Shay rubbed his forehead, feeling only slightly improved.

His father was a duke and was still alive. In this house.

"How did it come to be that my husband ended up alone and starving on the streets of Inverness if he is the heir of a duke-dom?" Thea asked smartly.

"Please accompany me to the duke's chamber so we might sort this all out together."

Forney looked at Shay as if to ask him if he was able to stand up and walk, and for the life of him Shay didn't know the answer. At least not until Thea slipped her hand into his and gave an encouraging squeeze.

"Come, my love. Let us go solve this mystery."

"The Case of the Lost Earl?"

"I do say, that has a ring to it, does it not?"

Shay chuckled and stood. Tucking her hand into the crook of his elbow he leaned down to press a kiss at her temple.

"It doesn't matter who I am or what name or title I shall claim. I love you, Thea."

She smiled and pressed her hand along his cheek.

"A name doesn't make a man. It is his heart that does that."

"My heart only has your name on it."

She pressed a hand to her stomach reminding him of the change coming. "For now."

"Aye, lass. There will be room," he promised.

Forney cleared his throat and Shay kissed his wife's knuckles taking an extra second to not only enjoy her, but to make sure the man knew Shay wasn't to be pushed about.

"Come. Let's go meet your father," she encouraged.

The duke's bedchamber was as dark as the rest of the house. It made the man look all the more pale against the burgundy counterpane on the bed. When his gaze came to Shay he looked as if he'd seen a ghost.

Shay could relate after having seen the painting downstairs. Now, seeing him in person, was even more disconcerting. Despite his poor health they looked so much alike as to be… well, what they obviously were. Father and son.

Shay had a father.

"It's him," the man said.

"It is, Your Grace. If he didn't look the spitting image of you, his wife wears the Glenlivet ring on her finger as further proof."

"It belonged to my mother," Shay explained.

"As it belonged to my mother before her," the duke said. He turned his attention to Forney. "Might be best to gather a few chairs as we have much to discuss and I don't want them hovering over me."

"Right away, Your Grace."

The chairs in the room were moved so they could converse with the duke easier and then Forney left the room.

"You must have as many questions as I do," he said with a chuckle that turned into a dry cough.

"At least," Shay admitted as he got up and poured the man a glass of water.

"Thank you, Ellis," he said and Shay jolted at hearing another person use that name.

"Perhaps it would be more logical to go in order of events. The duke can fill in the earlier years and then Shay—that is, Ellis—can fill in what happened after that," Thea suggested the plan after Shay and his father had been sitting staring at one another for a full minute.

God love his wife for her moving them along.

"Very well. But if I grow too weary, we may have to pause. My strength leaves me suddenly at times."

Shay nodded and waited for the man to collect his thoughts before he began to explain.

"Your mother and I were married off by our families. Though she loved another, I was going to be a duke and therefore a better match. I did try to make the best of the arrangement. It is not so easy to share one's life with a complete stranger, but I tried. For a while at least."

He coughed a bit and Shay worried that would be the end of the story for now, but the duke prevailed and continued.

"She, however, wanted nothing to do with me. We were at least fortunate that she got with child in short order. When you were born, she seemed more than relieved to have fulfilled her duty. She began seeing her lover in private, though not so discreet as she should have been for I heard about it from one of the villagers.

"Your mother was a faithless wretch, but in those days I was a drunken brute who was used to having anything I wanted. The two of together were much like tinder and a spark. But I never expected she would take you and run. She'd taken money and jewels, but it couldn't have been enough to keep her in the life she was accustomed to for all those years. I expected her to return at some point, but never heard a word. I found out the man she'd fancied had married another and then died. I knew she hadn't gone to him. It was as if she'd simply vanished."

"I'm not sure where we were in the early days, but we ended up in Inverness, living with her sister Deborah."

The duke interrupted. "I don't know who that was but your

mother had no sisters."

Shay thought that made some bit of sense.

"When my mother died, Auntie Deborah left me alone. I was six when I was put on the street. I found some other boys and we found ways to survive. Picking pockets and tending to horses when I was a bit bigger. There was never enough food, and winters were the hardest."

He went on to explain about Sheamus and his death. Explaining how he'd lied when Harrington came looking for the other boy. How all this time he'd been an imposter.

"It pains me to think that while I was warm in my home, my son went hungry and cold. I've had so many years to get over my anger with your mother. I'm sure she did what she thought was right. I can only think she worried I would hurt you. And I can't say whether that risk was real or not. I'm a different man than I'd been back then."

Shay took a good look at the man. Despite his ill pallor, he was not so very old. His hair had only begun to gray at the temples.

"I never knew anything of this life," Shay said. "When my mother was ill she gave me the ring and told me to keep it hidden and never sell it or lose it. She said it was very important. That I would need it one day. I thought she meant for when I would take a wife." He spared a glance to Thea. He'd never considered having anyone so lovely as her when he'd been living in a tiny cottage with his mother.

"I assume she thought it would prove who you were, not that I need to do more than look at you to know you are my son." He let out a sigh. "There is no reason for us to dwell on the past, for it is beyond our reach. If you gave peace to an old, dying man while assuring your survival than who can judge? But unfortunately there is the matter of your future and another old, dying man who needs some peace in knowing the dukedom will pass to his son."

Shay let out a breath and looked at Thea.

"I do believe Robert will have his task cut out for him in having to unravel all of this."

The duke chuckled. "I imagine you are not the first heir to come forward at the last moment to claim a title."

No. In fact, this wasn't the first time Shay had done just that.

"I do hope it is not the last moment. I'd like to have time to become acquainted," Shay said, not realizing how very important it was to him to know his father.

"We rarely have any say over such things. But I feel better than I have in months, having you here. I wish to know everything."

Shay cast a questioning look at Thea and as if she had read his mind she nodded.

"Maybe the first thing you will want to know is that you are to be a grandfather."

The man's blue eyes—the same color as Shay's—seemed to flare with excitement. He squinted in Thea's direction.

"That is a joy, but appears to be some time from now."

"Aye. We only just found out."

The duke gave a determined nod. "Then I'll have something else to hold on for. I won't want to miss meeting my grandchild."

"You will not," Thea said.

"Once the legalities are seen to, we can have you moved into Glenlivet House. There is a suite of rooms in the east wing that will afford a young married couple their privacy."

He must have noticed Thea's worried look. For the duke laughed.

"My dear, I would be grateful to you if you would see the house to rights. There has not been a woman's touch since my mother and I'll say while I never cared much about what color something was, now that I lie here all day looking at these bleak walls I find myself wishing for something with a bit more cheer."

Thea nodded.

"I will see to it straight away, Your Grace. Starting with a room for you with more windows I think."

Shay didn't know what to say as they returned to Buchanan House, and Thea was just as quiet in the carriage. When they were in their bedchamber they looked at each other and then she rushed into his arms as he held them out.

As they stood there in a steady embrace, he felt centered again, when the last few hours had tossed him out to rough sea. But Thea was the person who gave him strength to move on, whatever was to come.

"I feel I should apologize for ye were a marchioness this morning and now it seems you'll only be a countess."

She raised her head and smiled at him.

"I don't care about the title or even the name—for I already have two myself—so long as you are my husband I know I will be happy."

"No matter my name or title, I will make it so. Always."

Epilogue

Two years later…

"…THE PONY'S HOOVES lifted into the air as wings sprouted from his back. They were flying," Shay—or rather Ellis—read to their son.

"This new book by Flemming S. Buchanan is quite popular with the little ones," Thea said with a smile. After they had gotten settled in their new home, Ellis had some ideas for his own stories and Thea was happy to help him navigate the publishing world to see them printed.

Ellis winked at her as Forney pushed the duke into the room in his rolling chair. It was amazing how much his health had improved when Thea and Ellis moved in. Some days he was even able to stand and walk a small distance.

Thea had stripped the house of the dreadful green wallpaper and put up more blue and gray shades, similar to the décor at Cawdor Castle. She'd wanted her husband to feel at home there. With so many changes in their life it was comforting to have some things that had remained the same.

Their home in Scotland was not far from Cawdor and was as picturesque. But Thea and Ellis preferred Cawdor which they were able to keep. As no other Buchanans were found to take the title, the House of Lords determined the titles and holdings were to be combined.

To say Reese and Finn had been shocked by the news would be an understatement. They had not yet taken to call him by his new name, and Ellis wasn't bothered by it. It had been somewhat easier for Thea because she had already used his real name on occasion, but sometimes she slipped up as well.

When she did he often explained, "I am both men. I am Shay, the boy so frightened of dying that I lied about who I was for most of my life. But I am also Ellis Hayes. Deep inside where the Glenlivet blood runs through my veins. But whatever name I answer to, my heart is undeniably yours, Thea."

Her husband seemed free. Now that he wasn't hiding behind secrets and deception he was lighter and happier.

"I've not missed the ending, have I?" the duke asked. "It's the very best part."

Ellis dropped the book to his lap and tilted his head. "Do you think it's the best part because you truly enjoy the ending, or because you are amused when wee Sheamus insists on me reading it again?"

"Most definitely the latter." He didn't even pretend. Thea imagined that as a man aged he cared less and less about saying and doing the proper things. Since the duke claimed he was granted extra time he'd not expected, he'd practically eschewed all the rules of proper Society so he might have a bit of fun.

Something her husband and son enjoyed immensely, especially when they raced the wheeled chair about in the foyer.

"Geep," Shay reached for the duke. She and Ellis weren't sure why their son called him that, but it was clear who he meant.

"Hand over the lad," the duke ordered with a big grin that reminded her of Ellis's wide smile. "I shall finish reading the story to him. It is a lovely day. Take the countess for a stroll of the gardens, boy." Did the man wink at her husband?

Ellis chuckled and turned over both the book and their son to the duke who began reading right away as Shay settled comfortably in the older man's lap.

"Come wife, I'm told it is a lovely day for a stroll in the gardens," Ellis's mouth pulled up into a smirk.

"Is there something different about the gardens today?" she asked. "Since when does the duke force us to take air?"

"It is not about the air, love. He told me a few days ago how pleased he is to have a family and how much he would like to have a *larger* family." Ellis raised his brows in a suggestive manner.

"Larger? He wants us… in the garden?" Thea stammered.

"There are surely worse places. The garden is quite lovely. And private." That last part he said as he placed kisses along her neck. His head dropped lower and she paused a moment considering whether or not she should tell him.

Not being able to hold it in, she pushed him back slightly so she could see him clearly.

"Our family is already set to become larger."

"You're…?"

"I am. But that doesn't mean we should not take advantage of such a lovely day in the gardens."

He kissed her and then smiled. "It would be a crime not to."

THE END.

ABOUT THE AUTHOR

One very early morning, Allison B. Hanson woke up with a conversation going on in her head. It wasn't so much a dream as being forced awake by her imagination. Unable to go back to sleep, she gave in, went to the computer, and began writing. Years later it still hasn't stopped.

Allison lives near Hershey, Pennsylvania and writes Highlander Historical and Scottish Regencies.

Catch up with Allison on any of her social media platforms here:

Website:
allisonbhanson.wordpress.com

Facebook:
facebook.com/BlueRidgeRomance

Twitter:
@AllisonBHanson

Instagram:
@allisonbhanson

Goodreads:
goodreads.com/author/show/9860589

BookBub:
bookbub.com/authors/allison-b-hanson

www.ingramcontent.com/pod-product-compliance
Lightning Source LLC
Chambersburg PA
CBHW060356310726
48976CB00003B/847